DANCE, DIGGER, DANCE

a novel

Stephen Debonrepos

ISBN: 979-8-9999635-5-0

Acknowledgments

I wish to thank the wonderful L K
for her generous contributions to this book
as well as my crack team of beta readers:
Benjamin Bundt, Steve Goodie,
Lawanda Kharshiing Olin and Anandi de Jong.
But, most of all, I wish to thank my ace editor and one and
only,Nicole Brechka.

Table of Contents

Part I – Spain

Chapter 1- Stop! Thief!

He hadn't *set out* to kill anyone.

Digger stood in an outdoor marketplace in Andalusia, Spain, perched at the top of a flight of stone stairs. He was eighteen and travelling alone in the summer of 1985. Vendors lined the narrow aisles, their stalls bright with purses, dresses, and the smell of frying churros and simmering paella. Colors shimmered in the heat, and the mingled aromas curled around him like smoke.

"*Alto! Ladrón!* Stop! Thief!" a voice cried out.

He saw a commotion down below. Through the crowd, it appeared that the police were chasing a purse snatcher. They were approaching.

In a split second, Digger had to choose sides between the law and the criminal. After all, he *was* an art forger, a con man, and a double-murderer. The choice was made like a sneeze. The purse won out.

Digger scurried his lanky body down the steps and tripped the thief with a sweep of the leg. The man hit the ground hard, fumbling a knife that skidded across the pavestones. He lunged, grappling Digger's legs and sending him crashing to the ground. Digger grabbed the blade but was met with a brutal kick to the shin that made him convulse in terrific pain. In a wild, blind reflex, he thrust and wiggled the knife into the thief's ribs. They wrestled until the man weakened and went limp.

Winded, the police caught up. The crowd created a pocket around Digger.

"Self-defense!" cried some of the onlookers, a mix of locals and tourists. Others called for Digger's head. They grabbed his arms and jostled him until the police, blowing their screaming whistles, pried him away.

A few people attended to the injured man whose blood gushed out onto the stones despite their efforts to stop it. The police stood guard over them, holding back the crowd. After some valiant effort, a male bystander put his two fingers to the thief's jugular vein. The thief was dead.

An old woman wrapped in a shawl looked Digger square in the eye. *"No necesitabas matarlo. No tenías que matar a mi sobrino,"* she said in Spanish. *"You didn't have to kill my nephew."*

Digger looked in the direction the thief had been headed. Another man, bearing a resemblance to the one he had just killed, stood there still in the foot traffic moving past him, like a stone in a brook.

Digger knew that many pickpockets worked together, passing wallets several times before they had a chance to get caught. This accomplice in his sights stood for just a moment, then turned and fled.

The young woman—perhaps early to mid-twenties—was thrilled to have her Gucci purse back. She spat on the thief, whose face was now covered with somebody's scarf.

Digger picked up his sketchbook off the ground and he held it behind his back. Of its many sketches and doodles, a good number of them depicted the human figure in various states of disassembly. He didn't need the police taking an interest in his medieval ideation as they briefly questioned him.

The cops looked at Digger's passport, making an open-and-shut case of it on the spot, and let Digger go. It appeared that arresting Americans was bad for tourism, at least to these cops. (Digger's youth may have played a part in his swift and astonishing dismissal.)

The woman whose purse had been snatched spoke in crisp English to Digger, based on an accurate assumption. Yes, he was an American.

"Are you all right?" she asked Digger cautiously, as an ambulance arrived.

"Yes, *yo creo que sí,*" answered Digger. Having been born and raised in Southern California, bordering on Mexico, Digger was at least conversational in Spanish. His having an IQ of 160 didn't hurt.

"I should be asking *you.* Are you okay?"

She stuck her arm straight out, offering her hand.

"I'm Maria Lucia. Thank you for… taking that bastard down."

Digger was still reeling. He did not have an easy answer for how to sit in this situation. He had killed before, but this seemed so incidental, so casual and so *public*. His marbled feelings were tangled with the lifelong lessons of "Thou shall not kill" and the like.

The medics loaded the lifeless body into the ambulance while the aunt shuddered with tears and anger. She yelled something at Digger and climbed into the vehicle with her dead nephew. This didn't seem to faze the young woman.

"I'm to meet my brother Basilio for tapas in a half an hour and I *insist* that you join us."

She was, hands down, one of the most gorgeous women Digger had ever seen, with huge alert brown eyes and hair so black it seemed to suck in the light around it, a sort of inverted halo.

They took a cab toward town.

*

"So, you killed a man over the cash and make-up that my sister had in her purse?" asked Basilio.

Digger was an American tourist, and felt like a rather unwelcome poseur in Basilio's eyes. Basilio, late twenties, was not conventionally handsome, but had a roguish, carved quality that, according to Maria Lucia, fascinated women. His lashes were long. His body was tall, yet somehow compact, as if carved from a hardwood.

"Basilio! The man pulled a knife on Digger! The man could have killed him!" Digger liked the way she pronounced *heem*.

"So, tell me," Basilio asked, leaning into Digger. "Were you really fighting for your life?"

"Yes. Yes, I was."

"Well then, that's that." Basilio got up and went to the ordering counter.

"Don't listen to him," Maria Lucia said to Digger. "You know how painters can be."

"Basilio is a painter?" Digger decided not to point out the coincidence that he too was a draughtsman and painter.

"Yes. A very good one. In school, he was always getting kicked out."

Basilio returned with a fresh supply of tapas, skewered with toothpicks and served on small plates. He placed the

15

plates of food down on the table. Digger drummed his fingers on the table, still shaken by his all-too-recent killing, more so than he let on.

"Basilio. I don't know if I should eat more," Maria Lucia groaned.

"Come on! You're going to need fuel for the club tonight!" Basilio put his hand on Digger's shoulder with enough weight to take some of Digger's balance. "Come, Digger. Join us, as our guest." It sounded more like a pronouncement than a request.

At the end of the meal, they simply paid by how many toothpicks were left on their plates. Basilio smiled at Digger in a way that seemed up for interpretation.

Chapter 2 - Clubbing

The three of them, Digger, Maria Lucia and Basilio, strolled the merchant-lined streets, following the flow of traffic. According to Digger's hosts, it was hours before proper clubbing time, so the two siblings took Digger to see some of the city and to hear some romantic live Spanish guitar.

They entered a courtyard and sat down cross-legged on the cobblestone, beneath a stone gazebo with about thirty other listeners, a few in folding chairs. Oil lamps ringed around them.

Before the musician arrived, Digger and his new pals made friendly conversation with those sitting right next to them.

"So, Digger, what are you doing in Andalusia?" asked a student from Turkey, holding hands with a girl he said he had just met a week ago.

"You know, I haven't the foggiest idea," said Digger with a chuckle.

"Did you just throw a dart at a map?" asked Basilio.

"Not quite." Digger felt that he had insulted his new hosts. "I had just heard so many wonderful things," which was not a lie. Bridget, back in the States, had told Digger how much she longed to return to Spain.

The guitarist walked up and took his place and a quiet fell upon the group. He wore a white blousy shirt and black vest that had elaborate blood-colored embroidery and had a jet-black ponytail. He removed his flat hat and placed it, open side down, on the cobblestone next to him.

He used no amplification, so all sat hushed in reverence. He took his stool and quickly tuned his guitar before quietly naming the evening's first selection, *Romance Anonimo*.

Then, with an elegant flourish of the wrist, he began to play. His fingers plucked and slid, strummed and slapped. Notes rippled through the night air and through the audience.

He played nearly forty-five minutes, after which the crowd broke into soft but earnest applause. The performer then turned his hat open side up and stepped back as the people filled it with *pesetas*.

From the moonlight *concierto*, the three of them hailed a cab and went to the club.

It was unlike any club Digger had attended in the United States, not that he had a wealth of clubbing experience. The walls were brick and plaster with vaulted ceilings and wrought iron. Colored lights spun and flashed.

They waded into the center of the crowd and began to dance.

Maria Lucia kept her purse slung across her body. She and her brother raised their arms above their heads and moved to pop and dance hits, both American and European. For hours, Digger drifted further and further into a warm oblivion of motion, like a flag, waving in gusts of music.

Long after midnight, Digger heard his name called. It was from far away. He checked to make sure he wasn't hearing things. He squinted through the fog machine haze for a sight he just could not believe.

It was Perry. Digger hadn't seen Perry since grade school. Perry swam through the crowd, over to Digger. He still had those signature teeth and beach blond hair.

"They say that if you ever travel to Europe, you'll always bump into somebody you knew in the States, right?" yelled Perry with a pep that Digger just couldn't match.

Digger didn't really feel like being recognized right then.

"Yeah! They say that, alright!" yelled Digger.

"Small world, huh?" shouted Perry.

They shouted above the music until the song stopped and Perry found himself still shouting.

"We should keep in touch! You're in the book, right?"

Digger gave him a liar's thumbs up, then motioned that he had to get back to his friends. Perry nodded that he understood.

Digger danced until he had nothing left. He was damp and limp. He was sticky with sweat. He stood to the side and watched others dance for a while. Just a huge crowd of strong and vibrant bodies twisting themselves to the music. It could have been anywhere in the world, but it also couldn't. This was unmistakably Spain and this was an unmistakably Spanish crowd. There was a distinct dialect to their look and movements. The people were beautiful and the music was magic.

Then, a second wave of energy lifted him. Digger was wide awake and hyperaware of his wet clothing. A stranger put a small vial to his nose and told him to snort. Digger shook his head and mouthed the words, *"No, gracias,"* before dancing away and looking for Maria Lucia and Basilio.

Digger spotted them on a terrace outside, Maria Lucia blowing ornate columns of kinked smoke into the moonlight.

He made his way to them. The horizon was just beginning to hum with sunlight.

"Look. I don't know how far you two have to drive, but you can crash at my hotel room, if you like," Digger offered.

"Crash?" asked Basilio. "No, Digger. It is not time to crash. It is time for breakfast! Leave your hotel and come stay at our *villa* for the weekend."

"Your villa?"

"Well, it belongs to our father. You will love him."

Digger wasn't certain if that was a prediction or an order.

Chapter 3 - The Villa

As dawn approached, Digger, Maria Lucia and Basilio found then climbed into their boxy Fiat. They swung by Digger's hotel room, where he not only grabbed his two bags, but checked out.

Digger sat in the car's front seat, craning his neck in order to include Maria Lucia in the conversation. Basilio drove.

"So, then Pashone, the drawing and composition guru, is looking at Jonny's painting. And he says to him." Digger paused. "'You have a lot of good ideas—'" he began in his very best impression of the master.

Maria Lucia could see Basilio's anticipatory smile in the rear-view mirror.

"'But you're not using any of them!'"

The three of them burst into laughter.

The early morning streets were not as deserted as Digger had expected. A whole population who lived avoiding the Spanish heat were out and about, strolling, dining and people watching. Some walked small dogs.

Digger and his host siblings ate a light breakfast of coffee and pastries at an outdoor café, then they drove out of town.

The streets wound and thickened with trees as they neared the father's villa.

The lull in the conversation allowed Digger's thoughts to seep into his mind.

He thought about his departure from the States, how he fled what was likely only his own fear.

He had sold counterfeit Old Masters drawings and killed two people—now three— and had gotten away with all of these crimes. So far, that is. He needed to submerge himself in a foreign land and regroup. He knew that if was to be caught, it would likely be due to making a dumb mistake. He was here to prevent that mistake.

He needed some braking distance. He was a fugitive, in and of his mind.

"Ah, here we are," announced Basilio.

A lean older man with cropped white hair emerged from the house and greeted them, along with a shapely younger woman—late thirties, perhaps, who spoke with an Italian accent.

"Papá. You are looking well. This is our friend. *Se llama* Digger," introduced Basilio.

"*Mucho gusto, señor,*" offered Digger.

"Ah, your accent is very good. But, my English needs practice. Call me Álvaro. This is my wife, Francesca."

Digger made eye contact with Francesca then quickly looked away. He could hear his pulse in his ears. He needed to leave. He needed to stay. Francesca was going to give him trouble and he wanted to run headlong into it.

Soon, an elaborate spread was laid out on a large wooden table outside, beneath the shade of a few large trees. They all had a small "second breakfast," consisting of various breads and pastries, eggs and coffee. They sipped and nibbled. The conversation was limited to small talk until it had run its course.

"Too much!" said Basilio, standing into a morning stretch. "I eat too much!"

"And now?" asked Digger.

"Sleep!" exclaimed Maria Lucia. She showed Digger to his room where he toppled into bed.

Digger slept until 1 pm. He awoke, got up and looked for the others.

He found them lounging among piles of books and magazines of various languages in the library. Sitting on a recliner, Maria Lucia made her way through a large stack of papers.

"There he is! Pull up a book, my friend," said Basilio.

"Don't mind if I do."

Digger looked along the impressive shelves. He grabbed some art books. The texts were mostly in Italian, French and Spanish, but there were a couple in English and luckily he understood the images.

He found assorted relics—postcards, pamphlets and photos—all used as bookmarks. They held the place somebody found close to their heart. While turning the pages on a huge volume on Italian sculpture, Digger found a small photograph. It slipped into his lap.

He looked at Maria Lucia and Basilio. They were each in their own cocoon, shutting out the world around them.

Digger picked up the photo and studied it. It was of Francesca, hand on her hip, head thrown back with what looked like a huge laugh. It looked to be a few years old. He gasped, then without moving his head, he palmed the picture, slipping it into his right pants pocket.

With his senses on high alert, Digger attempted to rejoin his hosts in their activities.

They studied and read, sometimes bursting into small flames of conversations that died out just as abruptly.

"Hey, Digger. You want to see me beat Basilio's ass?"

Basilio sat up, intrigued, laying his philosophy book on his chest. "Surely, you can't be serious."

"Oh, but I am," answered Maria Lucia.

"Okay. Bring it."

*

The siblings had the badminton net up in no time flat. Digger sat on the grass, hugging his knees.

Maria Lucia held her racquet with two hands, shifting her weight from one foot to another in a wide stance.

"Did she tell you that she used to play in college?" asked Basilio playfully.

"No!" Digger laughed.

"Did he ever tell you that he talks a lot when he's going to lose?" taunted Maria Lucia.

"Okay, zero-zero." With that Basilio served the birdie into the air. It whipped across space, clearing the net by mere inches.

By the time it reached the opposite side, Maria Lucia had positioned herself solidly in front of it and, with a scooping motion, sent it high into the air, over to Basilio's side.

This rally continued with each of the siblings lunging and swatting, leaping and crashing, until a point was made. They continued the game until Basilio finally claimed victory.

"Okay, Digger. Now, is your turn," he said. "You must play the victor!"

"Oh, no. Not me. I'm not the sports type."

"Sports? This isn't *sports*. This is life and death!"

"Well," Digger got up, dusting himself off. "Alright then!"

Maria Lucia clasped her hands together in delight.

If Digger had a reputation as a non-jock, he surely earned it today. He covered his head from the incoming birdie, hit it onto the roof and swung repeatedly, making contact with nothing but air.

Basilio could not keep from laughing. He laughed so hard that he had to rest his hands on his knees and catch his breath.

"I can't breathe," wheezed Basilio, still laughing. "We must stop. Time for *siesta*—huff, puff—Digger—huff, puff—do you take a siesta in the United States?"

"Not officially," answered Digger.

Digger and Maria Lucia helped Basilio to another side of the villa.

They slept in hammocks and in chairs.

Eventually, a voice from afar called them to eat.

Maria Lucia, Basilio and Digger dragged themselves, stretching and yawning, toward the kitchen in order to wash their hands and faces.

They emerged outside into the zealous sunshine and took their seats at the table.

The food was again a feast.

"You eat like this every day?" The spread impressed Digger.

"Largely," answered Maria Lucia and Basilio's father, Álvaro.

"Mostly," corrected Basilio.

Basilio's father Álvaro was still a vibrant man, having sired a pair of twin children after his reaching sixty-four, with Francesca. The twins were the half-sister and half-brother of Basilio and Maria Lucia.

"When my husband is here, he works the garden," explained Francesca. "We usually take the children with us when we travel, although now that they are bigger, they're in need of more time at home base."

"Home base," repeated Digger, indicating that he was following her.

"Our house in Madrid. So, Digger," asked Álvaro, drinking his Tinto de Verano, "What is your gift? Everybody has a gift,"

"Drawing, I suppose."

"An artist! *Marvalloso!*"

Álvaro's two small twins, a boy and a girl, ran around the table, making play noise.

"Please, come. Stay here and teach art to my children," implored Álvaro. "They have tutors for reading, math, music and a few languages, but nothing for art. I will pay you well."

"Why can't Basilio teach his little brother and sister?" Digger asked. "Besides, how do you know I'm any good?" he said, munching on his toast with jam and drinking hot chocolate.

"Ridiculous," Basilio scoffed. "I have far too much going on than to be dropping everything every time he decides to start a new family."

"Please," Álvaro insisted, pleaded. "I am not an artist and I cannot bear for them to grow up without this education. Besides, Digger, I think you would enjoy it."

Digger chuckled, actually considering this offer.

"So, how did you meet?" Álvaro asked the general table.

All were silent until Basilio offered, "Digger thwarted a criminal who tried to snatch Maria Lucia's purse."

"Maria Lucia! Are you alright?" asked a concerned Francesca.

"I'm fine. It's all over with. I am absolutely fine."

Álvaro got a serious look on his face, as though about to render a verdict.

"You are okay, *mija?*"

"Absolutely."

"Digger, I have you to thank, then. I am indebted to you."

"Not at all," answered Digger.

Álvaro, however, seemed like a man who did not easily take no for an answer.

Chapter 4 - That Bastard American

People were bustling in the Andalusian square. Daniel the pickpocket found his mark, an American student, loud in his movements and attire. You could always tell an American.

He followed the student for a block or two. He bumped into the mark, carrying a folded newspaper to hide the action of lifting the student's wallet. Then Daniel quickly made his way to his cousin Pedro, who was standing at the ready, leaning on a building column. In a slick, invisible move, he passed the wallet to Pedro, and just kept walking briskly.

Pedro took off in the opposite direction.

After a short bit, Pedro would hand off the wallet yet again, to another accomplice. The student wouldn't realize that his wallet was missing until he reached for it next, trying to pay for his hostel bunk or his next meal.

That bastard American who had recently killed Daniel's brother, the purse snatcher Alejándro, was on his mind constantly. Daniel knew that he must have been a tourist and was probably gone by now, fled to the next stop on an economy tour or back to the States entirely. But he kept his eyes peeled on the slight chance, the tiniest chance that he was still around, for if he was still around, Daniel would kill him.

Chapter 5 - *Houshi*

"Okay, okay. I'll do it."

And so it would be. Digger would spend the Summer at the villa, teaching drawing and painting to Álvaro's small twin children.

"Excellente!" exclaimed Álvaro excitedly.

With that, Álvaro left Digger, Basilio and Maria Lucia in the study.

Of the three, Basilio, Maria Lucia and Álvaro, only Maria Lucia smoked. And boy, did she smoke. Two packs a day, easy, Digger guessed.

Maria Lucia was a writer. She had attended university in the States for her MFA. Basilio studied in France, but he did not complete. She was writing a book on Harper Lee and Truman Capote's strained friendship and planned to do another one on his later years. She had written a book on Gaudi when an undergrad in Madrid.

When Digger asked what Álvaro "did," the question was immediately diffused, laughed off. Digger got the distinct impression that they were fabulously wealthy, but not necessarily by legal means, or perhaps it was just in poor taste to discuss one's wealth.

The money he was paid was obscene and Digger saved nearly every *peseta*. It was deposited into an account in the Canary Islands.

"I am fatigued! We should go out on the boat," suggested Maria Lucia.

"Yes! And we should invite Proximo," added Basilio.

"Oh, no. Not that Proximo," insisted Álvaro.

Basilio laughed.

"Come, Digger," beckoned Basilio. "Let me show you my studio."

It was impressive, at least to Digger. It was a large room with large windows, plenty of natural light and inspiring views of the Spanish forest. The canvases—stretched and rolled—seemed limitless, as did the supply of tubes of oil paint. He couldn't count the big jars of paintbrushes. *One could paint his whole life*, Digger thought, *and never leave this house.* It was a cage that would trap Digger easily.

Basilio began to talk Digger through his paintings, the ones leaning against the walls.

"I'm no expert," began Basilio in all false modesty, "But this one, I am not happy with. It lacks the requisite tension for this sort of painting. You see the arm? It lacks power. I don't know what to do about it."

Digger held his tongue about this, didn't want to come off as some teenage know-it-all or stick his foot in his mouth revealing a *true* ignorance.

"You're like an expert curator. Of course. They're your paintings, right? Why wouldn't you sound like an expert?" Digger said, erring on the side of diplomacy.

"Many artists, in fact, are rather useless beyond their work," Basilio said. "The chores of talking about it in any meaningful way, well, they're incapable of performing them. Different set of skills."

Basilio peeled off his shirt and removed his pants, raising Digger's eyebrows. He then put on a pair of canvas work pants, all paint-spattered. He then laid an eight-foot square painting on the floor and began to scrub at it with a rag he had dipped in turpentine.

"How old are you, again?"

"I'm eighteen."

"Funny, you seem… older."

When he stood it back up, Basilio put his fist to his chin and became very quiet. He broke the silence by asking Digger, "So, Digger. What do you think? What does it need?"

Digger felt put on the spot. Was this some sort of test? Basilio seemed vulnerable, sincere in his asking. Digger felt pressured. He didn't want to say something just for the sake of saying it.

"That blue in the right corner, there," Digger began. "Seems a bit aggressive. And I would maybe soften this edge, here." He pointed along the left side of the canvas and looked at Basilio for his reaction.

Basilio took his time.

"Hmmm… You may have something," he finally said.

Digger was glad just to not be seen as some kind of joke by this guy.

Even though Digger and Basilio seemed to hit it off in the art studio, Digger knew that they weren't exactly peers. Basilio was more mature, experienced, knowledgable and confident. Whereas, Digger had an intuition that could be discovered and fed, but not grown without seed.

Digger saw what looked like a series along a far wall. He pointed to the four paintings.

"Are these for a show?"

"A show? Digger, what are you talking about?"

"You know, for a gallery." Digger had the distinct impression that he had stepped in something. "Do you think you'll ever 'make it?'"

"What? You mean become famous? You are concerned about such things?"

"Well, yeah, I guess. In the States, a lot of pretty influential people say that painting is dead." Digger wished he had kept his mouth shut.

"Well, then they are dead. I am not painting for them. I am painting for me. I am painting for... well, for *painting*." Basilio turned toward an open window, then to Digger. "I am on my path. It is not for show. I am pursuing ideas that haunt me. There is a word, Digger. It is Japanese. The word is *houshi*. It is doing something like chopping wood or fetching water, without praise or reward. You do it because it must be done."

Chapter 6 - *Chango*

The following day, Maria Lucia banged away at her Smith-Corona word processor, surrounded by haystacks of research. She had photocopies of exhaustive correspondence, journal entries and itineraries, although how well her book was coming was anybody's guess.

She reached what she considered a reasonable stopping point and stretched in her chair, ready to call it a day. She got up and left her office, looking for Digger. She went outside.

Shirtless Basilio was throwing knives at a wooden target.

"Basilio! Have you seen Digger? I want to take him on a hike!" she yelled.

"A hike? You'll miss supper!"

"We'll be back in plenty of time, Basilio. *Como chingas,*" she snapped.

Maria Lucia eventually found Digger. He had just finished helping Francesca move some boxes in the cellar. He said that he was game for an outing.

Maria Lucia wore an impossibly wide-brimmed straw hat and large Jackie O. sunglasses.

She and Digger made their way through the meadow, leading away from the villa.

She picked up a stick and used it to swat at the tall grass.

"So, Digger. You have a girl back home?"

"No."

"You should. You're young."

Digger shrugged. "You?" he asked.

"No. But, I was married once. I did it in the States when I was in college. *Ay,* did my father throw a *fit.* I was nineteen and stupid." Maria Lucia continued to swat at the grass."I just love the smell of these trees."

She left the path and approached one of the giant trees. She buried her nose in its trunk and drew in deeply. She then let out a sigh.

"Come, Digger, you try."

Digger imitated her actions precisely. The sweet smell was surprising to him. He expected something much more like a Christmas tree. He leapt up and caught a branch. He then swung his legs forward and wrapped them around the trunk. Digger pulled himself up into the tree.

"*Chango,*" she called him. Monkey.

He scaled the tree for a few minutes until he rested on a branch, near the top.

Digger liked seeing Maria Lucia down there, looking up at him and holding her hat on her head.

He climbed down and they resumed their march toward the crest of a hill.

At the top of the hill was a clearing. From there, Digger could see quite a distance, all of the lush land below.

"Thank you for saving my purse, Digger." She stared into the lush horizon. "How do you feel about it?"

He didn't want to answer truthfully. The truth was that Digger was absolutely fine with it, that he had made notes on how he'd do it differently if given the chance to do it again.

"I'll be fine."

"So brave."

Chapter 7 - Yacht Party

"We are ready to go, yes?" asked Basilio. The boat's engines were already rumbling.

"We are still waiting on Proximo," answered Maria Lucia.

Basilio was clearly not pleased with this update. Álvaro, Francesca and the children stayed back at the villa. This was a yacht party for young adults.

Then, a smallish figure came bounding down the pier toward the boat.

"Proximo!" yelled the friends.

Proximo was met with slaps on the back and shoulders as he boarded the yacht.

Digger expected more rocking, but the boat felt as steady and solid as land as it pulled away from the stone dock. He leaned against the railing and watched the Port de Rosas shrink into the distance.

He thought that it might have been a good idea to wear sunblock, but that never seemed to occur to anyone else either.

Since arriving in Spain, Digger had seen some sights, killed a man and made some rich friends. And now, he was cruising on a private yacht, just off the Port de Rosas. There, Digger met more rich folk. There were Maria Lucia's and Basilio's four friends—Rafa, Luis, Elena and Blanca. Then, there was Proximo.

Proximo was a slight man in a blazer and neck chain. He seemed like the kind of person who was always up to something, as if he had an angle. He sized Digger up and cornered him, as if he sniffed something on Digger, his nature.

"You look like someone up for a little action. You want to make some money?" Proximo spoke in hushed tones.

"Doing what?" Digger was intrigued but played it cool.

"It's safe. Completely, totally safe. 100%."

But, Proximo looked like a guy used to getting caught. Anybody talking seriously and so casually with a complete stranger must be a total fool. And, despite his curiosity, Digger's foolishness wasn't total.

Digger did a lot of nodding and listening until he excused himself from present company and went in search of a drink. He bumped into Elena.

Elena had short hair the color of mink and wore large round sunglasses. She was petit and spoke terrific English. They all did, to varying degrees. These were beautiful educated people. Digger had a burgeoning thing for her.

Digger procured himself a Pellegrino and took a swig, marvelling at Elena's face.

"Your English is excellent," said Digger.

"So is yours." Elena threw her head back in laughter. "You Americans, so isolated, speaking only English. Here, in Europe, we have to learn to get along with our neighbors. I don't like to stay put in one place. I like to travel. When I go to Paris, I speak some French. When I'm in Berlin, I use some German."

Somebody wanted to go in the water. "Come on! Jump in!" they yelled.

"Come, Digger. Come swimming with us!" Elena enticed.

"But, I haven't brought a suit!"

"Bah! You don't need a suit!" With that, Basilio peeled off his shirt and stepped out of his shorts and underwear. He extended his hands in a *ta-daaa* gesture, then went to the railing where he jumped off to the shrieks of his sister and friends. Rafa and Luis followed suit as if they were in a race.

When Elena pulled off her clothing and climbed down the ladder to the launching ramp, completely nude, Digger's eyes nearly left his head. He immediately disrobed, forgetting any trace of self-consciousness he might have had. Only Maria Lucia opted to disappear, only to return in a scandalous one-piece swimsuit and climb down to the ramp, before leaping forward in a dive into the jewel blue water.

They swam and they splashed. They gulped and they spat. They stroked and they floated, taking turns only to sun on the deck of the boat, some on lounge chairs, some on the landing ramp.

Digger closed his eyes and thanked whatever god might listen, to not have an erection at this particular time, partial as he was to the completely nude Elena, let alone Blanca, in her black ponytails.

He grew hot and dozed off.

As Digger slowly emerged back into that particular moment, he saw blood vessels and sun spots through his eyelids. His skin crackled with fledgling sunburn.

"Oh, no! Digger!" exclaimed Elena. "You are all crispy!"

Digger's pain limited his responses to Ah! and Ah! Ah!

"Let me get you some aloe vera." Elena ran off, returning later with a plastic squeeze bottle. "Here. I found this in the first aid."

Elena then told Digger to hush and began applying the flecked gel onto his raw skin, causing him to wince and flinch.

They were still very much nude and she avoided no part of his body.

She made a soft cooing sound as she spread the goo all over him, which Digger found a very mixed blessing. On the one hand, there was the contact and undivided attention with, and of, Elena. Then, there was the lobster boil sensation of being served with a New York strip steak.

Digger could hardly take it.

He wanted to make conversation, but remembered what his old figure drawing teacher, Walt, taught him about the etiquette of dealing with models. One didn't compliment a model on their body while they were still disrobed. Besides, talking about her looks would just be so stock, so *obvious*. So, he kept his compliments to himself.

"So," began Digger, without a backup plan. "Do you… like art?" *That was original.*

"Absolutely. But, I am a poet, you know."

"Really? Could you recite something?"

"Oh, no. I write to be read. Not to be heard. Besides, I only write in Spanish."

"Your poems must be beautiful."

"Why? Is it because you think I am beautiful?"

"No. It's just that your movements are so elegant, so crisp. Nothing wasted. And your clothes. You have great taste—"

Just then, Elena kissed Digger on the shoulder.

"Everybody!" called someone in a rallying cry. "Time to eat!"

They all scrambled into their clothes. An enormous picnic basket, the size of a large baby stroller, was heaved out into the seating area. It contained cheeses, Spanish chorizo, fruit, breads, wine and other dried meats.

They ate boisterously, laughing, singing and dancing.

Somebody pulled out a guitar.

"Toca! Toca!" they all began to chant. Play! Play!

Finally, Rafa collected the guitar and tuned it.

Digger poised himself to hear some romantic, traditional, maybe even Flamenco guitar music. But no. Rafa began playing the opening riff to *It Never Rains in California,* to the delight and applause of the group.

"Rafa knows I love this song," said Blanca as she doot doo doo doot-ed along.

Rafa went through a repertoire of American pop that included Eagles, The Beatles, The Rolling Stones and many, many others. Elena and Bianca put their heads upon each other's shoulders as the sun hung low in the sky, streaking it with pinks, oranges and gold. They drank wine and cognac until very late.

Surprisingly, the yacht would accommodate everybody comfortably.

Not long after saying their goodnights and turning in, Elena turned up in Digger's bunk. She slid in wearing her day clothes—khaki shorts and an expensive designer tank top—and curled up next to him. She snuggled her head on his chest and purred herself to sleep. Digger also slept, eventually.

***

The next morning, Digger woke and climbed to the deck. Elena was gone.

"Good morning!" Digger said to Basilio, who was making coffee in a huge, commercial machine. Basilio put his finger to his lips, shushing him.

"Too early to be chipper. Coffee first."

The guests rose from their bunks like swamp gases. They moved in slow motion, each grasping at the air for cups of coffee. They eventually drifted into place around the breakfast table.

"What time is it?" asked somebody.

"It is hangover o'clock," answered somebody else.

Digger nodded a good morning to Elena who gave him a smile too knowing to be bashful.

Mimosas flowed and conversation thawed. Chuckles crashed into laughter.

Thus began another day of splashing and sunrays.

At the end of the day, they pulled back into port. There were hugs and double-kisses.

Digger wanted Elena's telephone number but, a) didn't know how the game was played over here in Europe, and b) had no idea if she was just out of his league. She could be some heiress or princess.

Who knew?

Chapter 8 - She Likes You

"Digger, Come. It is time to paint," Basilio commanded.

These words hit Digger like a splash of water. He put down the book he was reading and followed Basilio out of the plush comfort of the villa library and toward his painting studio.

"You know, Elena. I think she likes you," said Basilio, laying his large, square painting on the floor.

"Get outta town," said Digger, playing half-dumb.

"Yes. I think you could be good together." Basilio peeled off his shirt.

"Think so?" Digger also peeled off his shirt, carefully, revealing his lean, modest, still sunburned, chest.

"Sure. She is highly intelligent, a marvelous poet, highly educated with a beautiful soul, and you… You know what they say, opposites attract."

Basilio gestured for Digger to select a canvas to paint on. Digger chose a stretched canvas about two by three feet.

"Gesso?" asked Digger.

"Over there. On the bottom of the trolley," Basilio indicated with a forefinger. "So, Digger. The eternal question—What are you going to paint?"

"The eternal answer—I don't know!"

Digger covered the canvas with gesso, using a paint roller. He then grabbed a large paintbrush and began brushing a herringbone pattern on wet surface.

"Why are you doing that? You already have the roller," asked Basilio.

"I prefer the brush texture. I know that either of them will just smooth out on their own. It's just a preference."

Basilio made a *not bad* face and Digger placed his closed hand over his mouth in thought.

"What to paint. What to paint…"

Digger then dashed out of the room. When he returned, he had a sketchbook in hand.

"Ah, yes. Use compositions from your sketchbooks. You are like Goya," observed Basilio.

When he looked over Digger's shoulder, he saw Digger's gruesome depictions.

"You are *very much* like Goya."

They painted together for hours until Basilio said, "If you'll excuse me." He grabbed his shirt and left. Digger assumed that he went to make a phone call, but no. Basilio was gone for quite a while.

The shadows in the room shifted with the movement of the sun.

Even after an hour, Basilio didn't return. Digger decided to look for him.

He found him sitting under a tree, reading a book.

"Hey, where'd you go?" Digger asked.

"Why, I went here."

"You could have told me."

"Do I need your permission? Your blessing? You were so in the moment, Digger. I did not want to break your concentration." Basilio looked at Digger with absolutely no expression. "Come. I'm starving. Let's eat."

45

They had missed the main meal with the family, so Digger and Basilio made sandwiches in the kitchen of Jamón Ibérico and manchego cheese on a crusty focaccia-style bread. They washed this down with green bottles of cold Alhambra beer.

"Have you been to the museums, Digger?"

"I haven't been anywhere," Digger chuckled.

"This seems to be true!" laughed Basilio. "You need to go. It's important for you to go. You have a gift, Digger. Don't rely upon it. You must learn. You have plenty of work to do."

Digger chewed his food, listening intently.

"Tomorrow. Take the car. Go. Go to the museums."

Digger nodded.

"I'll have Elena meet you there."

Chapter 9 - Personal?

Digger walked in a wide circle where Basilio told him to meet Elena, in the crowded square in front of the museum. He had arrived twenty minutes early for their 1:00 pm date. It was now 1:40.

Finally, he heard a voice.

"Digger! Digger! *Aqui!*"

It was Elena.

She had a smile that could sharpen diamonds and a nose that belonged on a canvas. Her short, mink-like hair shimmered in the sun. She wore sunglasses, a hat and a light scarf.

Digger looked sharp in jeans and the suit coat he had made for the art forgery swindle in the States earlier that year. Although now, it seemed a lifetime ago. A whole person ago.

"Here." She handed Digger a ticket. "I got them in advance so we wouldn't have to wait."

They made their way to the thickly crowded line and into the museum.

"So, is this your first time here, Elena?"

"Oh, no. I have been coming here since I was a child," she began, deftly pivoting to flattery, "but it will be nice to come this time with a painter!"

This comment pressured Digger even more than before. Not only did he see her as slightly older, more educated and refined, not to mention likely wealthy, but now he was being put in the position of painting authority when his own knowledge of art theory and history was so scant. He also knew this couldn't be the first time she had been here with a painter. Perhaps this were a test, a test of how well he could discuss art. Perhaps, she just meant to boost his confidence. All he knew was that he wished they had gone roller skating instead.

They entered a large room filled with masterpieces and Elena zeroed in on a huge one.

"Come, Digger! Let's go!" Elena took his hand and pulled him along.

"*Las Meninas*, Ladies in Waiting."

"Diego Velázquez," Digger contributed, silently grateful to see one of the paintings he actually knew.

"I just love how the artist included all of this behind-the-scenes stuff, the self-portrait, the back of the canvas..." Elena trailed off.

"You know what I love," Digger began, "was the way he let the brush stroke stand. He didn't fuss with excessive blending."

Elena leaned in, surprised and delighted to hear Digger's engagement in the conversation.

"He mixed his colors so well, so precisely, that he painted his subjects in tile-like sections, letting the eye blend the colors. When we look closely, we see his bold strokes."

"Very nice, Señor Digger. Very nice."

"Why, thank you, Señorita Elena."

They milled around, strolling past the masterpieces with no particular order or plan.

Elena stopped in front of one.

"Ah, yes. *The Nude Maja.* I dismiss the rumors of who the model was. I don't care about her class. I don't care if she was Goya's mistress or not. I just love her open pose and direct gaze. Goya painted this sixty-something years before Manet's *Olympia*."

Digger nodded along, listening to her every word. Elena seemed to appreciate his attentiveness. She continued, pointing to the next painting.

"Now, here we have *The Clothed Maja*, where all the clues lay. Here, we get the clothing, rich with detail about the model's station in society. I dismiss it all."

Digger chuckled. "'Nuff said!'

They wandered a bit more, saying very little. Again, Elena took his hand, but this time not to yank him to the next room. No, this time it was quiet, a tender gesture. They clasped and quietly made their way to their next masterpiece.

"Goya's *Saturn Devouring His Son*," Elena announced. It was a nightmare image of an insane looking man, eating the head off a smaller figure. Both Digger and Elena stood there, held by the painting's ghoulish spell. "Critics have long interpreted and refuted this nightmare work." Elena leaned back as she spoke. Digger leaned in.

"Wow. This is when he really gets personal," said Digger reading the placard next to the painting.

"Personal?"

"The guy painted it on the wall of his house. He didn't mean it for the public. He meant to live with it."

"He had to have meant something. This is just too dark to be his private thoughts."

"Oh," said Digger with a grin, "These are his private thoughts."

Elena seemed agitated by these words. Perhaps she found them just a little creepy. She released his hand.

"I'm hungry," said Digger.

Elena hardly spoke at lunch. She answered Digger's questions, but politely, not with great engagement. Her eyes suddenly flashed.

"Hey! I have an idea."

The bookstore was made up of cinder blocks and creaking boards bending under the weight of their loads. Books were stacked to their tipping point. Walls of paperbacks threatened to topple onto their patrons. Small Post-It notes told Digger what language section he was in. There were books in Spanish, books in French, in English, Arabic, German… You name it.

Shoppers shimmied sideways through the narrow canals that ran between islands of books. The place smelled of old paper, leather, ink and glue.

Digger and Elena made their way around the store with their heads cocked sideways so that they could read the titles on the spines.

Elena pursued the "English" section, where she found a paperback copy of *Even Cowgirls Get the Blues.*

"Oh! Tom Robbins! I love Tom Robbins. Here. Digger. Let me buy this for you."

This was an abrupt change in attitude. Probably, just a concession toward diplomacy.

In the same section, Digger found a copy of an American graphic novel, *Love and Rockets: Music for Mechanics.* He brought it with him when they made their way to the cashier.

They checked out and went outside.

On the street, Elena handed Digger his gift.

"Here. I hope you enjoy it."

Digger handed her his purchase. Elena took it out of its bag.

"What is this? A comic book?"

"It's a graphic novel. It's like a comic book, but most graphic novels have a beginning, middle and an end, like a movie. Most comics, on the other hand, are like soap operas. They go on forever."

Elena just blinked as Digger continued, more embarrassed by the word.

"Aren't you a little old for superheroes, Digger?"

"You see, this isn't about superheroes. It's about these two girls, Hopey and Maggie…"

Digger trailed off after watching Elena's eyes glaze over.

"Anyway. It's for you."

"Thank you, Digger." Elena looked around her. "It's getting late."

"I have a car. I could give you a ride—"

"That's okay. I'm good."

Digger walked back to the car Basilio had loaned him with his hands in the pockets of his jeans, muttering all the way. He drove the picturesque streets and roads back toward the villa, hoping not to get lost.

He had really blown it with Elena. Or, had he? He was just being himself. At least, a very true *part* of himself. If she didn't like him, that surely was nobody's fault. Then, why did Digger feel so ashamed? He tried talking himself into feeling better, but it was no use.

Basilio was chopping firewood when Digger pulled up. The sun had disappeared but the sky still glowed orange.

Digger tried to avoid him and wanted to just go inside the house, but Basilio called to him. Digger walked toward him.

"So, how did it go at the museum?"

"Well. The Goyas were particularly—"

"Not the museum, *pendejo.*" Basilio hoisted his ax high overhead. "How did it go with Elena? Did you get a kiss? Are you going out tomorrow?" He brought the ax down splitting the section of log.

"No."

"No, what?"

"No, neither."

"No, neither? You must have really blown it. She said she was crazy about you."

"Well," Digger began, rather miffed to have to have this conversation *on top of* having such a disastrous ending to a date, "That's the way the cookie bounces."

"Hey, hey! Don't be so defensive. I was merely… following up." Basilio stuck the ax into the log. "Here, help me gather these."

Digger helped Basilio gather the chopped firewood and stack it against the ivy-covered wall. He felt like a child. He felt like a stooge. He did not feel like having a meal.

Through the window, Digger saw Francesca in the kitchen and felt something within him expand and tighten. He excused himself and went into the kitchen where he asked Francesca if he could be of any help. She accepted his offer and put him to work, all under Basilio's watchful eye.

Chapter 10 - Older Meat

A couple of days later, the stuff arrived.

Delivery men wearing ordinary clothes arrived in a pick-up truck and backed it onto the gravel driveway at the villa. They unloaded boxes and put them where Digger pointed.

Digger ran to his room to fetch his wallet, his mind scrambling to figure how much to tip. After all, they *did* have to drive a ways out into the Spanish jungle to make this delivery. But, by the time he returned with his wallet, the truck was coughing its way back down the driveway.

In addition to his pay, which still embarrassed him just a little, Digger was given a stack of cash to get anything he might need to teach little Pablo and Paloma.

Digger had thought about just asking Basilio for some of his art supplies, but then thought better of it.

He thought it best to go with kids easels rather than adult full-sized ones, since they were, uh, kids. Digger had no idea what to do with this. *How did I ever get myself into such a situation?*

Nervous and, frankly, with very little idea of how to proceed, Digger opted to take advantage of the perfect weather and teach the kids outside.

He unboxed and assembled a few wooden easels, then opened and inventoried the rest of the boxes. There were pencils, varieties of pads of paper, charcoal, acrylic and oil paints, pastels, paintbrushes and little stools.

Digger sought out the kids, finally ready for them. No dice. They were nowhere to be found.

Digger looked for Francesca.

He found her under a tree, in a field, nearly fifty yards from the house.

He asked about the twins and Francesca put down her book and pointed farther down the field. It was there that he saw them. They were in the company of a *burro*, a donkey. Paloma doubled over in laughter, her hands on her inner thighs. Pablo jumped and danced, carrying a stick.

Francesca called them in. "Paloma! Pablo! Come inside! Is time for you lesson!"

Digger brought the twins to the outside area that he had arranged for them.

They sat on their brand-new little art stools. They stared at their brand new little easels, then at Digger, who, in turn, stared back at them.

"So…" began Digger.

Pablo stretched while Paloma stifled a yawn.

"So, do either of you like to draw?" Digger asked. "Do you color?"

Nothing.

"What do you like?"

"I like donkeys!" squealed Paloma.

"Great! Why don't you and I start drawing some donkeys! And what about you, Pablo?"

"I like *musica*!" Pablo squealed.

"Okay, kid. You got me there. I like *musica*, too." Digger clapped his hands twice to get their attention.

Digger then, suddenly struck by something close to inspiration, jumped up and left the kids. He went to Álvaro's library and grabbed a couple of large books of photographs. He flipped until he found a picture of a donkey. He also picked up a Tin Tin comic book from the dining room table. He then popped back outside with the kids and placed the picture book on a music stand he liberated from Basilio's studio, securing it open with some C-clamps.

"Okay, kids, let's draw this donkey! Pick up your piece of bar charcoal."

The kids giggled when they saw the charcoal dust get all over their hands.

"You get started and I'll start too." Digger sat on a chair and drew on a full-sized easel he had *borrowed* from Basilio. He felt nervous and awful. He had no earthly idea what he was doing.

"Okay, now. That's a great way to draw a donkey. You're using lines to draw the donkey. That makes this a line drawing." Digger picked up a coloring book of "Las Aventuras de Tin Tin."

"Just like Tin Tin."

"Now, pick up this orange. Go ahead. Pick it up. Look at it. It's not flat. It's *round*."

"It has no line around it. Sure, we can *put* a line around it," Digger drew a circle on his large pad. "But that would make it a cartoon orange, wouldn't it?"

The children nodded.

"Let's look at this not like a flat Tin Tin orange, but like a round real orange!"

Digger then continued to demonstrate on the large paper pad.

"Now we're making little strokes, very lightly, like you're petting a kitty. We go round and round lightly, *slowly* making the orange."

The children dutifully copied Digger's actions, making gentle circular strokes on the paper.

"See how the orange has a light side? And a dark side?" Digger scraped the side of his bar charcoal to give shade to half of the round shape he had drawn.

The twins nodded enthusiastically, as one does with a discovery.

"Let's draw the orange, then we'll draw Tin Tin, then we'll draw Tin Tin the same way we did the orange!"

They looked confused.

"One thing at a time. Let's draw some fruit!"

The kids worked on their still life oranges silently, occasionally letting out a sigh.

Francesca came to ask when their lesson would be over, because they would all eat after.

"What is good for you, Francesca?"

"Half an hour. Half an hour is good for me." Her crooked smile was a handsome one.

*

Digger watched Álvaro turn the meat on the huge outdoor grill.

"Today, we are going to eat ox," said Álvaro, nearly salivating.

"Ox?" asked Digger apprehensively.

"*Sí.* Older ox. Younger meat is tougher. Older is better, *más rico*. The meat came from a neighbor, Pascual, just up the road."

The chop was bigger than any Digger had ever seen. It sizzled and spat as the flames licked the fatty edges. Occasionally, it popped when a piece of the fat exploded. It was like something from The Flintstones.

"You will like it. It has a lot of flavor."

Francesca called everybody for the afternoon meal. She laid out some of neighbor Pascual's homemade wine and her own homemade bread. Digger rose from his seat and asked if he could be of any help, following her into the kitchen. Francesca had him ladle out bowls of bean soup. He carried the bowls out to the table, two at a time, while she filled a *jarra,* an unglazed ceramic pitcher, with water.

Francesca, Álvaro, the twins Pablo and Paloma and Digger all sat at the large outdoor table.

"So, Digger, how are *mis hijos* doing with the arte? Will they soon be able to paint my portrait?" Álvaro joked, cutting himself a piece of cheese from a large wedge.

"Soon! Álvaro, Soon!" replied Digger.

The twins ate olives off their fingers.

Maria Lucia showed up.

"Maria Lucia!" Francesca asked sharply, "Where is your brother?"

"How do I know? I am not his jailer. Check his studio."

"Go and get him," Francesca commanded.

With a joking groan, Maria Lucia set her book down on the table and left, heading for the wing of the ivied house that contained Basilio's painting studio.

"Go on, Digger, *come,* eat," directed Francesca.

"I think I'll wait 'til everybody gets here."

"Ah, the boy shows respect!" said Álvaro.

The two siblings arrived, Basilio buttoning his shirt after painting bare-chested. They seated themselves at the table.

Francesca said, "Shall we give thanks for our guest?"

Álvaro responded, "I have no god to thank for this meal or anything else! Where was god when we were fighting Franco?"

Pablo waved a piece of cheese in the air. Paloma kicked her feet, staring straight up.

"Okay, fine. Digger, would you like to give the blessing?" asked Francesca.

"I'm afraid I—" Digger stammered, as he didn't consider himself a person of faith. In fact, he was raised a de facto atheist. His parents thought that anybody believing in those fairy tales was an ignorant, yet functioning, fool.

Yet, surrounded by all of the good-naturedness around him, Digger changed his tune. "I would be honored." Digger lowered his head and improvised. "Let us give thanks for this day, for the bounty of this food, for these good friends and for our time on earth."

"Amén!" There were scattered "Amens."

"So, Digger. I hear you are painting with Basilio," initiated Álvaro.

"You should see what this guy is painting. He's like Goya. Powerful stuff. Very political," described Basilio.

"Political?" said Digger, astonished.

"Yes! The dismembered bodies that represent—"

"Those bodies don't represent anything political, Basilio. They are just compositions that come from my imagination. My studies are completely free of politics."

"Art without politics? Can there be such a thing?" asked Basilio. "The personal is only that of the personal citizen, no?"

"No. It's of the person, me. That's it," answered Digger.

"Where is the power in such art, then? Does that just not make you another psychopath?"

"Perhaps. Is there still value in my art?"

All eyes looked to Basilio. He broke his bread in half.

"Not to me. Sorry,"

The table went into commotion, with voices saying, "Oh, come on, now" and "That's ridiculous."

They finally settled down.

Álvaro leaned forward on his elbows, his hands laced together.©

"The entire family will only be in the villa through the end of the Summer. That's when I, Francesca and the children will return to the main house in Madrid. Basilio will remain here and Maria Lucia will resume her apartment in Barcelona," Álvaro explained. "Digger, I invite you to follow the twins and me to Madrid and continue their lessons. You would have your own apartment and I would continue to pay you a handsome salary." His unblinking eyes stayed trained on Digger.

"Wow. That is quite generous of you, Señor Álvaro," Digger answered, stunned. "I will have to think about it."

Álvaro did not seem pleased with this delay in Digger's acceptance. "Let's change the subject!" Álvaro now had a twinkle in his eye. "You know, I know two children who play the violin *y la guitarra*." Álvaro's words made the children squeal with excitement. "Pablo, Paloma, how would you like to play for *Señor* Digger tonight?"

The twins talked over each other, slapping the air with their hands.

Everyone pitched in on the cleanup after the meal. The children stacked plates, using both hands. Maria Lucia picked up the stacks of plates and brought them to the kitchen. They were a well-coordinated ant farm.

After dinner, Digger helped Basilio wash dishes, while Francesca and Maria Lucia shared a cigarette outside. The sun still hung high in the Spanish sky.

"Digger, you know, you are very good with children. Have you thought about becoming a teacher?"

"Not seriously."

"Think about it," Basilio commanded.

Basilio wiped his hands dry with a towel and then tossed it to Digger.

Digger wanted to ask Basilio if he really saw no value in his art, but that smacked of a neediness that he was not yet ready to admit to.

They left the room.

Everybody met in the cozy sitting room where each took their place, Maria Lucia and Basilio on the sofa, Álvaro and Francesca on the love seat and Digger on a footstool. The chairs were left empty.

The twins, Paloma and Pablo, marched in carrying violin and guitar cases, respectively, along with leather portfolios and sturdy black metal music stands. They had their mother's deep brown eyes and wavy black hair. Paloma's heart-shaped face was a little Valentine, while Pablo looked like a little Rudolph Valentino.

"The twins, they play violin and guitar. They both play a bit of piano. They started when they were three," Álvaro announced proudly.

The honey sun was now low and gave the children just enough light over their shoulders to read their sheet music.

Paloma raised her bow and locked eyes with Pablo. Both raised their chins, then bounced them simultaneously, launching into Stanley Myer's *Cavatina* from "The Deer Hunter."

Francesca's hands were clasped the entire time. Maria Lucia had a tight grin on her face. Basilio was deadly serious, as if memorizing each note. Álvaro split his time with his eyes open and closed. Digger was charmed into submission.

When they finished their final note, the room broke out in applause, not loudly, but definitely in earnest.

The children followed with *Romanza* and finally, Bach's *Air on the G String*.

"Bravo! Bravo!" Álvaro yelled. The children just beamed for a moment, then they put their instruments into their open cases that lay upon the floor and ran to hug their parents.

"Go dress for bed," Francesca told the children. "You can still stay up for a little while, just go get dressed."

"I am going to light a fire," announced Maria Lucia.

"Maria Lucia, it's summer," scolded Basilio.

"*I want a fire.*" And a fire she made.

Álvaro poured cognac for the grown-ups. Digger was still getting used to being one of the "grown-ups."

Digger thought of a young woman he saw on the pier on their boat trip and how he'd like to tie her up.

"Digger, you look lost in thought. What are you thinking?" asked Francesca.

"Oh, just art stuff."

Álvaro didn't need much lubricating to get him telling stories of his youth. Anecdotes about Maria Lucia and Basilio as children followed.

"They didn't really play *with* each other, but they always played *near* each other. You couldn't find one without the other being too far away," Álvaro recalled. "Basilio was very protective of his sister. One time some kid at school shoved Maria Lucia and she fell down, hard. Basilio beat. the. hell out of that kid!"

Francesca recalled times from her own childhood in Cosenza.

When the invisible Bowie knife was passed to Digger, he told about how he traded nude male drawings for food to a waitress.

"That is brilliant!" proclaimed Basilio.

It was now late. The yawning began and each person said good night and shuffled to bed.

Chapter 11 - *Ropa*

Digger unloaded his clothes from the washer and put them in the dryer.

Maria Lucia walked in, carrying a full laundry basket.

"Digger, you keep wearing the same things over and over. Don't you own any clothes?"

"Just what you see," answered Digger.

"Tell you what. You and I are going shopping."

It was still quite early in the day. Digger thought that clothes shopping just might be the welcome adventure he needed.

An hour later, Digger and Maria Lucia climbed into the Fiat and took off for town.

She took him to a high-end part of town that he had never seen. It was like Rodeo Dr. in Beverly Hills, but somehow, much more stylish, chic.

They got out of the car and Maria Lucia locked it.

The two of them walked among the elegant people, strolling as if in a fashion show.

They entered a Louis Vuitton store.

"Here. These are good," said Maria Lucia.

She snatched a selection of shirts from the racks and handed it to Digger.

He went to a changing room to try one on. *Man! These are nice!* He looked at the price tag and gulped. Wow! A hundred bucks a piece. *You get what you pay for, I guess.*

Next, they looked for some pants: some jeans, some trousers. Digger dropped over two grand in that store alone. Luckily, he still had his student credit cards from Design Center on him. He wasn't sure about tapping money from his new international accounts yet.

Later in the afternoon, the two of them took their many shopping bags and headed for some ice cream. They purchased two cones and spotted an open table. While walking to it, Maria Lucia broke her heel, twisting her ankle. She yelled out in pain and quickly lowered herself to the ground.

"Are you alright?" asked Digger.

"I think so. It doesn't appear to be broken. It just hurts. Can you help me back to the car. It's not far from here."

Digger helped her to her feet and surprised her by hoisting her up onto his back, piggyback style. She cackled the whole way back to the car, waving like a rodeo cowboy. Digger managed to carry her along with all of the shopping bags they had accumulated.

Maria Lucia fought Digger on the issue of going to the hospital, but Digger insisted.

They wound up in a clinic. Maria Lucia's ankle was checked out and wrapped. She was given a set of crutches and sent on her way. Digger drove them home to the villa.

"Oh! What happened?" asked Francesca upon seeing her step-daughter hobbling out of the car and toward her.

"Digger and I went out to play," joked Maria Lucia.

"Too much of a good thing, I guess," said Digger.

Francesca folded her arms as the two passed her by, filing into the house.

Chapter 12 - Chiaroscuro

The children were eager for their next art lesson. They bounced in place and chattered nonstop. This time, they sat at a picnic table covered in butcher paper. Digger had laid out two bowls of fruit, a box of Conté crayons and drawing pads.

Digger let them draw whatever they liked as a warm-up. They drew carefully. They drew spastically. Circles, flowers and cats. Airplanes, dancers and donkeys.

He pulled out his own pad of paper and drew a straight line.

"What is this?" he asked, pointing to the line.

"It's a line!" the children answered in unison.

Digger picked up an orange and said, "I'm going to draw an orange." Digger picked up his Conté crayon and drew a circle on his pad, next to the straight line.

"If this is a line," he began, pointing to the straight line, "What kind of drawing is this? Remember from last time?"

Each kid raised a forefinger, excitedly.

"You don't have to raise your hands."

"A *line* drawing!" Paloma blurted out.

"Right. And Pablo, if I color this in,"—Digger laid in a tone—" is this line drawing solid?" Digger asked, shaking his head, "Or is it *flat*!" he said, nodding his head in a huge motion.

"It's flat!" yelled Pablo.

"*Claro*!" said Digger. "You got it!"

"Now, if I put the orange on the table, it has a light side," Digger pointed to the half of the orange in the sun, "And a darker side, a side in shadow, right?" He pointed to the shadow side.

"Yes!" they yelled.

"That's exactly right! We have a light side and a shadow side, so I'm going to *darken* this half here, right?"

"Right!"

Digger then darkened roughly half of the drawn orange.

"Does the orange cast a shadow on the paper on the table?"

"Yes!"

"Well, I guess I'd better draw that, then!"

Digger drew an elliptical shadow shape extending from the drawn orange.

"There! Do you think you can do that? Do you?"

"Yes!" They dutifully copied his example.

Digger drew alongside them, demonstrating and guiding them. After they had drawn a few oranges, they started drawing other things with shadows.

Paloma drew a donkey with a shadow. Pablo drew his mother, with a shadow side to her face as well as a shadow cast on the ground. She held a basket of laundry on her hip.

He let the rest of their time just be a free-for-all. The kids made jokes that had no punchlines, but cracked them up nonetheless.

"Why did the elephant?"

There was uproarious laughter.

That was a joke.

"The lady lost her hat!"

A laugh riot followed. *That* was a joke.

Digger had a blast, really enjoyed their company, but it looked like their hour was up.

When Francesca came to collect the children, they complained that they weren't done yet.

Digger felt the same way.

Chapter 13 - I See You, Digger

Basilio had invited Digger to throw knives with him. He led Digger to the clearing where a large wooden target stood. It was about fifteen yards away from the small table that he used to splay his throwing blades. Basilio took a couple of apples from his pockets and placed them there also.

Thok! Thok! Basilio threw them hard and they stuck deep, making a thick sound. Thok!

He hit bullseyes most every time.

After throwing all five knives, Basilio walked to the target and pulled them out with some effort before returning to Digger's side.

"Okay, Digger. It's your turn. The first thing you must do is count off your steps."

He led Digger to the rectangular, man-sized target where he told him to pace off from the target back to the throwing line. Digger complied.

Now, they were both back at the throwing line.

"You seem to create a lot of excuses to bump into Francesca, Digger." Basilio looked to the target. "How many paces? Come on. How many?"

"I'm sorry. I seem to have lost count."

"That's too bad. With the number of steps, you can estimate how many revolutions the knife will spin. This will determine whether you hold the knife by the handle or by the tip of the blade. I have looked in your sketchbook. You have quite a few sketches of Francesca. There is one in particular. I am very familiar with the photo that it is based upon. You have a very good memory to draw that. Here, Digger. It is your turn to throw."

Digger took the knife and listened closely to Basilio's instructions. The knife was long and bulbous, coming to a point. It had no sharp edges.

"Tell me, do you masterbate to it? Her image I mean," said Basilio.

Digger threw the knife. It spun toward the target and slapped it flat against the surface. It made a Pang! sound as it bounced off into space.

"Not bad," said Basilio. "Digger, do you think I could hit an apple from the palm of your hand?"

Digger regarded him with gunfighter cool. Dark thoughts crossed his face like storm clouds. This was a man who wanted to keep his options open.

"Trust is a mysterious thing, Digger. What is it that you distrust? My skill or my intention?"

Digger took the apple off the table and walked it to the target.

"She is my father's wife," Basilio said. "True you are but a sapling and she would never give you a second look, but it's not her I'm talking to, not her I am concerned about. My father likes you, Digger, but as you know, things can change."

Digger met Basilio's stare. He held the apple in his outstretched palm.

"I see you, Digger."

Basilio wound up, then threw the knife.

It exploded the apple.

Chapter 14 - No Lollipop Trees

For the children's next lesson, the child-sized easels were placed in the shaded clearing near the outdoor dining table at the villa. Digger went over all of the tools and materials, making certain that he hadn't forgotten anything.

Right on cue, the five-year-old twins came skipping and yipping into the clearing, clasping their hands excitedly. Digger helped the children into little smocks, so that they wouldn't get paint all over their play clothes.

"Today, we are going to paint. How does that sound?"

"I want to paint!" exclaimed Paloma.

"Let's paint!" seconded Pablo.

They stood outdoors at their easels, painting the trees with tempera on paper, just as Digger had done in elementary school.

Pablo improvised a barn in his picture. Paloma stuck a *burro* in hers, but mostly the kids stuck to painting the trees. Digger figured now was the time to just let them get some mileage exploring with their brushes.

The children relied mostly on outlines, as most children do. They would delineate a shape, then fill it in, like making a coloring book. This was still "thinking flat."

The kids pumped out a few masterpieces that Digger placed on the large outdoor dining table to dry, with stones on each corner, lest they blow away. They had lollipop trees, M-shaped birds, a mutant donkey and a box barn.

It was time for a break. Digger had them gather around while he demonstrated at his larger easel. He dipped a paintbrush into a bottle of green tempera paint and then swirled it onto a paper plate.

"What color is this?" he asked the two.

"Green!" they shouted in unison.

"That's right! But when I look at those trees, what do I see?"

The children looked at the trees in the distance.

"Do I see one green or do I see lots of greens?

"Lots of greens!" the children yelled.

"That's right! Why, I see lots of different greens!" answered Digger. "I see light greens, dark greens. I see warm greens, cool greens. How do I get those different greens?"

Digger looked to the twins for an answer.

"I mix blue and yellow!"

Digger scraped some blue paint onto a paper plate and added yellow. He swirled it around until it yielded a freaky, streaky green color. The twins reacted with delight and awe, respectively.

"The greens you mix are better than greens from a bottle. See how beautiful the streaks of different shades are?"

The kids oohed and ahhed.

"Look! We can make our own orange! And, purple!"

"The color of royalty!" shouted Paloma.

'That's right!" Digger affirmed.

"Digger, how do you make red?" asked Pablo,

"We can't make red. I'm sorry. We have to just use the red, out of the bottle."

"Oh, I wanted to make red," said a dejected Pablo.

"Next lesson, we're gonna make a whole color wheel, showing all of the colors and how to make them!"

The kids looked at each other as if Digger had told them a secret. A color wheel!

"*Guau!*" said the kids.

They all got back to painting. Digger had them stop holding the brush like a pencil and start gripping it like a knife so that they could cover large areas more easily.

Gradually, their stab stabbing motions became more controlled, more deliberate strokes.

Digger painted alongside them. The tempera paints were clumsy and muddy. This wouldn't do. He would have them use acrylic paints next time.

Digger felt a rush of pride watching the children mixing their own greens, purples, oranges and muddy browns.

They weren't just painting lollipops, tree symbols. They were painting the tree in front of them. They were starting to paint what they *saw*. They were beginning to *see*.

Álvaro came over to check in on the kids. He looked surprised to see them so focused and industrious. They must have looked more serious than he had anticipated. He felt confident. He had made a good decision, bringing Digger aboard. He hoped that it would last.

Chapter 15 - Up to the Elbow

Digger closed his sketchbook and thought about Francesca. He attempted to invent a reason for seeing her as he roamed the villa, seeking her out.

Could she help him find X? Would she assist him with Y?

He stopped at the doorway to the kitchen. Through the window, he could see her pull up in the Fiat. She parked not far from the house.

Digger sauntered out to greet her as she exited the car and neared its hatchback. He saw groceries inside the car.

"Could I help you with these?" he asked as she popped the rear door.

"Why, that would be wonderful!"

He made quite the effort of carrying the bags in, two at a time, briskly and efficiently.

She thanked him and mentioned that she was ready to start cooking dinner. Digger volunteered to assist.

"Are you sure? Do you know how to cook?"

"I have some knife skills," Digger responded.

"Very good, then."

She went to the sink to wash her hands and Digger sidled up, right beside her. He put his hands into the water running from the faucet. Francesca was using a bar of soap to lather up her hands and arms, up to the elbow. When she saw what Digger was doing, she took his hands and began to lather them up, all the way up his forearm.

"There. That's better." Her Italian accent was thick, undoing Digger's composure. He quietly panicked, fearful that somebody would walk in and disrupt their little scenario.

"Now scrub," she ordered.

Digger complied. His hands scoured each other as he washed to the elbow like a surgeon. He offered to chop vegetables and she thanked him.

"Oh, it's my pleasure."

Digger set to chopping the mounds of onions, garlic, tomatoes, bell peppers, eggplant, zucchini, and potatoes for the meal. Francesca began to prep two large chickens.

"Oh, these feet. They ache," complained Francesca. "I have been on them all day."

Digger took in a deep breath.

"I could rub them for you," he offered.

"What?"

"I could rub them for you, massage your feet."

For an instant, Francesca's face accepted his offer. But then her features settled themselves into a more cautious arrangement, as if to say, *Did I hear him right?* "No, Digger. That's quite alright. They just need some soaking."

Digger felt exposed. He thought he'd make a hasty apology or an excuse to dismiss himself, but then he remembered the advice his mother had always given him, even if it were in a manner of scolding.

The first thing to do when you find yourself in a hole… is to stop digging.

Digger would just push forward with his kitchen chores as if nothing had happened. Move along. Nothing to see here. *These aren't the droids you're looking for.*

Some staff from the family's main house in Madrid showed up to help Francesca with this grand, last meal at the villa for the summer.

Digger dismissed himself.

Chapter 16 - Never Fingers

Summer was winding down. The family sat down to their final feast together. The staff Álvaro brought in from Madrid to help was putting the finishing touches on setting the large outdoor table.

"I can't believe what I'm seeing with my little kids!" Álvaro exclaimed. "I wasn't expecting much more than a babysitter to get them finger painting, but, holy shit!"

"No, no. Never fingers. Only brushes," said Digger with a broad smile.

"I saw some of their artwork," said Maria Lucia, settling down at the table, no longer on crutches. "Amazing."

"I must admit surprise. I did not expect for you to produce such results so quickly with such young children."

"I love their paintings, just love them," said their mother Francesca with her fingers laced together.

Plates of food floated onto and off of the table. Wine glasses were filled and refilled. Digger's iced tea never reached bottom.

The leaves gently fanned their guests in the darkening shade. Children made jokes that ground conversation to a halt. Many *remember whens* now included Digger.

The attendees at this table would be breaking like billiard balls, each going off toward their post-summer destiny.

Chapter 17 - Digger Spotted

Digger went into town for the day. He had a touch of cabin fever from staying in the Villa for so long. He strode the city streets of Andalusia and just let the people, their hairstyles and their clothing stroke his eyes. The shops displayed fashions by local designers.

Just then, he was spotted by the old woman who had cursed him earlier in Andalusia, after the purse snatching and subsequent killing of her nephew. She was now accompanied by two men, one young, the other looked to be the pickpocket brother of the man Digger killed.

She pointed at Digger and the chase was on.

Digger ran and the one who looked like the slain thief's brother chased him while the younger man stayed with the old woman.

Digger darted and dodged. The man sprinted and weaved, snarling all the way.

"American bastard, I will kill you," he snarled in Spanish.

Digger spotted a woman getting out of a taxi. He hopped into it and told the driver to hit it, *pronto*.

The man let him get away. He kicked at the ground.

In the cab, Digger huffed and puffed, puzzled. He thought he'd left those guys far across town. *Well, criminals get around*, he thought. *Yes, we do. Yes, we do.*

Digger caught his breath and told the cabbie to take a loop around the block before dropping him at his car. He may have escaped, but he realized it was best to leave town, lest the goons follow him back to his rich friends and their kids. There was no way he could stay here in Andalusia. He would accept the job in Madrid.

Chapter 18 - Gustavo

Digger showed up at the Mansion in Madrid by taxi. He had with him his two pieces of luggage and a sketchbook. He was greeted by a well-muscled, mustachioed man in a tight-fitting, peach-colored Izod polo shirt.

"Señor Digger! Welcome! I am Gustavo. I have been expecting you."

This struck Digger as truly surreal, like a Spanish "Fantasy Island."

"I have been instructed to take care of your every need as you get settled in here at the main house."

"*Mucho gusto*, Gustavo. Your English is great."

"So is yours," Gustavo joked with a dentist's dream smile. "Here, let me take that for you."

Gustavo took Digger's bags before he could object. "Please, this way."

Digger followed Gustavo.

The ceilings of the main house were high enough to fly airplanes in. The elaborate, scrubbed-fresh tilework was a thing of museum-level beauty. Curved staircases coiled around to the left and right of the grand foyer as Digger and Gustavo entered, then traversed the belly of the main house.

Uniformed servants criss-crossed their path many times, carrying perfectly rectangled piles of towels or just briskly getting themselves from *aquí* to *allá,* here to there.

Digger noticed a slightly plump, young staff member whom he found quite fetching. She quickly looked away when they made eye contact. Gustavo noticed this.

"That is Maya. She will be bringing your clean linens." Gutavo returned to matters at hand. "I apologize. The taxi driver should have perhaps delivered you directly to your apartment."

It was quite a walk. Gustavo led Digger out of the side of the main house and down a wide walkway, through a meticulously groomed lawn. The side of the main house was draped in ivy.

They finally arrived at what looked like a little storybook forest clearing. It had the shade of surrounding trees and two small buildings. Digger was curious about the buildings but didn't ask. Gustavo seemed to need no prompting when it came to offering relevant information.

"And this, Señor Digger, is your apartment. This unattached building you see next to it was used as a workroom and for storage. It has been cleared out for you to make your studio."

"For teaching the children."

"No, no. Little Pablo and Paloma will be taught in the main house. This is for your own work and enjoyment."

Digger shook his head slightly. "It's a lot to take in, Gustavo."

"Let me tell you something. I have worked for *la familia Téllez* for over twenty-five years."

Digger quickly tried to guesstimate Gustavo's age based on this admission.

"And," Gustavo continued, "you will never find people who will take better care of you—"

Digger's shoulders relaxed and he felt a small smile pull the corners of his mouth.

"So long as," Gustavo completed, "you take good care of them."

To Digger, this sounded perhaps vaguely sinister. *I killed a man for trying to kill* me *while snatching Maria Lucia's purse. What do these people want from me?*

As they approached the Spanish cottage that was Digger's new digs, Gustavo handed him a set of keys.

"Go on," Gustavo said with a smile. "Open it."

The interior of the apartment was astonishing. It had its own furnished living room, kitchen, bathroom with a clawfoot tub and separate shower, and a bedroom with its own patio. The linens were new and the place smelled faintly of fresh paint. There was food in the fridge and a working telephone.

Gustavo looked at Digger with pride, as if he had done the whole thing with his own two hands. A thought just occurred to Digger.

"Gustavo?"

"Yes?"

"How often do Maria Lucia and Basilio come here to visit?"

"Sadly," Gustavo said, pursing his lips, "not as much as we would like, now that they are older.

This news saddened Digger. He was going to miss his new Spanish friends.

"Come!" Gustavo continued, "Let me show you your studio space."

Now, the studio. *That* smelled like fresh paint.

There was an industrial sink and two large trash cans, but most of all a gorgeous twenty-by-thirty-foot, concrete-floored workspace, an entirely blank canvas for Digger to design any way he chose.

"I can send for you for dinner, *la comida*. You can eat with the family until you settle in and start making your own plans," informed Gustavo. "As you can see, the driveway comes right behind your apartment. You will park there, come and go as you please, completely unmonitored." Gustavo bent a little at the waist, dismissing himself. "I'll let you unpack, freshen up." But then, an additional thought seemed to occur to him. "Oh, and your car will be ready tomorrow."

Digger was stupid for words. All he could come up with was all he really needed.

"Uh. Thanks?"

*

"*¿Vas a vivir con nosotros*, Digger?" asked Pablo.

"Are you going to live with us?" repeated his twin sister, Paloma, in English.

The formal dining room was set for six, Álvaro and his wife Francesca, the two children, Digger and a handsome woman in her early fifties whom Digger had never seen. She wore a blouse and slacks, a sharp, professional outfit. Her shoes looked expensive.

"This is my lawyer Sonia," introduced Álvaro.

"*Mucho gusto*, Señor Digger," said Sonia, bowing her head across the table.

"*Me encanta*, Señora Sonia," replied Digger, rising from his seat just enough to give a slight bow to her. His reply raised her eyebrows. It would be considered more affectionate than appropriate for a business introduction. She was, after all, Álvaro's *abogada*, his attorney. She did not seem to be in the market for a young American suitor, so she just returned her attention to her client, Álvaro.

"Yes, she is helping me sort out some business," Álvaro explained.

By now, the family was speaking quite a bit of Spanish with Digger, only using English when they wished to practice it for their own pleasure or benefit. They would sometimes combine the two languages within a single sentence.

The food was served and Digger hung back in the conversation, only answering questions and offering thanks and compliments on the feast that they all were consuming.

"So, Digger. That's an unusual name," observed Sonia.

"I'm an unusual person." Digger was going for more charming than cheeky, but wasn't sure that he wasn't fighting a losing battle.

"Many artists are known by nicknames. El Greco, Bronzino, Tintoretto, Botticelli…" Álvaro pointed out.

Digger wanted the spotlight taken off him.

"What kind of lawyer are you?" he asked.

Sonia and Álvaro looked at each other.

"The expensive kind," they responded in unison, laughing.

A soup was placed in front of each diner. Digger scooped up a spoonful, away from himself, as he had learned from the movies.

"Whoa! This is … chilled."

"Gazpacho! You have never tried gazpacho before?"

"No sir."

"So, Digger, tell me about your family," asked Sonia, in a soothing tone.

"I was raised by wolves."

"Come now."

"My mother sells real estate in the United States and … my sister works two part-time jobs."

"No, Digger. What kind of people are they? What kind of person is the woman who gave you life, who raised you?" asked Álvaro.

"Is she nice?" asked little Paloma, waving a butter knife like a windshield wiper.

"Uh, sure. She could be nice. She's smart. I'll tell you that. She started teaching me to read when I was two."

"That's like us!" exclaimed Pablo. "We started reading and playing the piano when we were little."

Álvaro looked skeptical. Usually, people spoke of their parents' character with great pride and detail and here Digger was, being flip and evasive.

Digger was also skeptical. Exactly what kind of lawyer was she?

"How do you find Madrid?" asked Sonia.

"I just got here, really."

"Have you seen the Church of Almudena?" asked Sonia.

"No, not yet?"

"Have you been to the bullfights?"

"I like bulls," interjected Pablo.

"We should not fight them," added Paloma.

"I haven't really done any sightseeing. I don't really want to see myself as a tourist, I suppose."

"More of an expatriate, eh, Digger?"

"Yeah, more like that."

After finishing their meal, Sonia urged Digger to see the sights. After all, he was in Madrid. Why else would one be in Spain?

Chapter 19 - Setting Up Shop

The next day, Gustavo helped Digger put the twins' studio together. Their father Álvaro didn't want their art materials brought from the villa. He wanted that stuff to remain there for their periodic visits. No, this was to be started from scratch, which was fine with Digger.

Digger just loved art supplies and could spend an eternity staring at catalogues and lingering in aisles of stores that sold thousands of varieties of pencils and paper.

He made a contract with himself. There would be rules.

The children would always use paint using brushes, never their fingers. Digger had purchased a book on art materials and their hazards in preparation for his teaching gig. (Before, he had felt just qualified enough to teach them how to draw hand turkeys, but wanted to change all of that.) It was called "Art Hardware" by Steven L. Saitzyk. In the book, he learned that "non-toxic" didn't mean "not dangerous." It only meant that one wouldn't die by ingesting a bunch of it at once. The insidious substance could still cause effects like neurological damage or cancer through prolonged contact with the skin. Kids should never fingerpaint.

Digger supervised as easels and tables were brought in by delivery men and placed wherever he indicated.

They'd started in the late morning and now it was early afternoon and most everything was done. All was stocked and arranged.

After dismissing Gustavo—the delivery men were long gone—Digger just stood there, admiring the space. He loved art studios, the way each configuration was unique, each employing and inspiring different ideas for storing supplies as well as artwork. Each workspace has its own personality.

The walls left plenty of room to hang the children's work as well as inspirational posters. There was a rollaway dry-erase whiteboard for lecture notes and small tables for still lifes.

There was something truly empowering about this moment. This was Digger's opportunity to not just complain about how things *should* be done, but to put his money (Álvaro's money, actually) where his mouth was and do things the way he thought they should be done.

When Digger was a kid in grade school, the teacher instructed the students to draw a tree. Digger did his level best to approximate the magnolia climbing tree in his front yard. When the teacher saw it, she held it up to the class, saying, "No, no, no." She then instructed the kids to watch her up at the chalkboard where she drew what looked essentially like a lollipop. "This," she explained, "is how you draw a tree." Digger's tree was wrong.

Now, he had his own students, not the summer camp situation he had at the villa, but real full-time students. *It is a big responsibility*, he thought to himself.

Digger would do everything differently. These kids would love him. If they didn't, why, somebody would have to be wrong.

Chapter 20 - Prowling Madrid

The following day would be Digger's first day with the twins in Madrid and knowing this made him anxious. The idea of taking the car the Téllez family gave him out for the very first time at night wasn't ideal, but he would go stir-crazy if he didn't get out.

Digger got into the two-year-old Porsche 911 Turbo and started her up. Its rumble added a new dimension to the weirdness of his current living situation.

Luckily, Spaniards drove on the right side, just like in the United States. Digger could just imagine himself smashing up if he had to drive on the left-hand side like they did in England. He depressed the clutch and put the vehicle in reverse. The car jerked as Digger acclimated to the Porsche's sensitivity.

Digger babied the clutch again and put it in first gear. He pulled out onto the small rivulet driveway that fed into the larger main driveway and drove away from the house and toward the heart of the city.

He parked the car on the street. It felt good to be a pedestrian in Madrid. Los Angeles punished those without cars. Madrid rewarded them.

Digger walked the kinked grid of city streets until seeing a sign for a flamenco show.

He never had any interest in flamenco dancing before, but he was never in Spain before, either. When he stopped to think about it, it really blew his mind.

A year ago, he would have never thought he could afford to see any part of Europe. Then again, a year ago, he had never taken a human life and now, for better or worse, he had. He had in fact, something of a running tally going and wasn't sure if these killings were just an isolated period of events, or the shape of things to come.

What if I had been caught for killing Dini Topp? Is that still possible?

This was why he was in Spain. He needed time to sort this all out.

He no longer wanted to be the old Digger, powerless and at the mercy of his intense and often violent feelings, reactions and appetites. Yet, he had a good idea what trouble he could get into by indulging his darker thoughts. He had been lucky, so far. But luck doesn't last and talent breeds cockiness.

Digger purchased one ticket for the 11:30 pm show and set himself adrift, wandering in front of the box office until the show started.

He drifted for a bit, realizing that he wasn't *people watching* as much as he was being *people watched*. Digger seemed to magnetize the eyeballs of passersby. He did not blend in well. He stuck out.

Digger enjoyed the buskers, the street musicians who played for donations. One wrapped up a simply gorgeous ballad only to follow it with a rousing, flamenco-style cover of Culture Club's *I'll Tumble 4 Ya*.

It was forty minutes 'til showtime, so Digger headed back.

By the time he arrived, a line had already formed. Hoping he wasn't somehow penalized for wandering off, he jumped into line immediately until he was told that the line was not for ticket holders. With this new information, a delighted Digger walked right in.

He sat at a small, round table. A server asked him, "Party of one?"

"A party? Hardly," Digger joked to no effect. The server took Digger's extra chair away.

Another server approached him.

"A drink, señor? Sangria?"

"Not right now, thanks."

"It is included with the show. Once the show starts, I doubt you will have another opportunity."

"You don't serve iced tea, do you? I don't really drink much."

"Why, of course, señor. I be right back."

Digger wondered if, since they served iced tea, this was a tourist trap.

The announcer came out. There was no raised stage, just a designated square of parquet wood floor.

The server returned with Digger's iced tea as soon as the round, sweaty announcer started barking his monologue. He encouraged *palmas*, clapping along with the dancers, as well as shouting "*Olé!*"

The pre-recorded music began, so loudly that Digger wished he hadn't been seated right next to a speaker.

A couple of Americans were in the audience. They yipped and whooped a bit prematurely.

The dancers came out. The lady had shiny black hair lacquered to her head and a dress that exploded in ruffles. She had a cosmetically applied beauty mark on one cheek. The man had hips as sleek as a switchblade and a short mop of wavy black hair.

They began to stomp and circle each other, clapping to the music by one ear.

This is good iced tea, Digger thought. *Man! It is loud.*

The venue was small, so leaving early without being noticed was out of the question. Digger just sat there, imagining blood trickling down his ear.

He stayed through the end.

The show wasn't as long as he had anticipated. Digger glanced at his watch to give the impression that he was late for something and left after stuffing a bill into a tip jar that was passed around.

Digger wandered out farther and farther from the main streets.

He walked down a street that was not as well-lit and with few shops. It had plain walls and a great number of women in short skirts and high heels standing or strolling about.

"American, you have girlfriend?"

Digger stopped walking to answer the woman in the too-tight outfit.

"No."

"Would you like a date?"

"No," answered Digger. He gave her face a closer look. "Your nose…"

"Yeah?"

"It's exquisite."

"No. You are making a joke," the woman said, skeptically.

"Do you have any makeup on you?" Digger continued in excellent Spanish.

"I have lipstick."

"Got any eyeliner?"

"Let me see." She checked her small purse. "Here. You want to put this on? Is that your kink?"

Digger liked the way she said *keenk*.

"Here."

Digger took the eyeliner and drew a few contours on the wall. She looked both ways and covered her mouth at his cheekiness for committing graffiti out in the open like this. She then recognized herself in the markings he was making on the wall.

Other prostitutes began to gather. "Lola! Look! It's you!" cried one.

Soon, there was a small group of women admiring the minimalist line drawing with the red lips.

"That," Digger stated, "is your nose."

"Could you do me?" asked a woman wearing fishnets.

"You mean draw you?" answered Digger, cheekily.

"Sure."

"Oh, I think I had better get out of here before the police take me for vandalism."

The entire group of women burst into laughter. How absurd to be in the company of prostitutes, worried about getting caught for making graffiti.

Digger thought he had best be on his way, so he made his way back toward the car that he would be soon calling his.

Chapter 21 - Contrapposto!

Early next morning, Digger hunted through the main house looking for Gustavo. He asked a maid who pointed him toward the endless backyard, where Gustavo was directing some landscapers, waving his muscular arms.

"Gustavo, for our first lesson in Madrid, I want to start the children on drawing and painting from live models. Might you know where to hire any?"

Gustavo thought this over. His mustachioed mouth went to one side as he scratched his chin.

"Would any of the house help do?" he asked.

"I'm sure they would, but would they do it?" responded Digger.

"It is no problem. Just let me know when you need them," Gustavo smiled, with that million-dollar smile.

Later that day, when Digger got to the twins' art studio, house staff Carmen and Marcos were already there. Each wore their staff uniform, Carmen in a powder blue sleeveless housecleaning tunic, Marcos in a powder blue short-sleeved shirt and khaki trousers. They looked like they were trying not to let on that they were nervous.

"Thank you for coming, Carmen, Marcos," Digger said in Spanish.

Each gave a weak smile and a little nod of the head.

The children scampered into the room.

"Carmen! Marcos!" They greeted their long-time servants. The staff members seemed increasingly confused. Were they to remain clothed? Were they to pose?

"Okay, kids! I have a special treat for you. Today we are going to start drawing from life!"

Pablo and Paloma looked at each other and their eyes got wide with wonder.

"Carmen and Marcos," Digger announced.

Carmen and Marcos tensed up at the mention of their names.

"Will be our models today! Okay, kids. Let's warm up."

With that, the kids launched into freestyle drawing, just doodling or sketching whatever they wanted. Paloma doodled owls and a donkey, whereas Pablo just set his marker whirling, making a colossal tangle of a single, continuous line. Carmen and Marcos just looked at each other.

Digger banged his hands together and the kids stopped drawing.

"Let's get ready for our demo. Carmen?"

"*Sí?*"

"Could you put your hand on your hip, please?"

Stiffly, Carmen obliged.

"Now, could you please put all of your weight on that leg?" asked Digger, demonstrating the pose.

Once again, she obliged, clearly disoriented.

"Marcos, take five."

Marcos also obliged, looking relieved.

"Alright, kids. Gather 'round."

The children clustered around Digger who sat in a chair with a large drawing pad on his lap.

"Now, today is all about messy drawing!"

"Messy drawing?!" the kids shouted.

"Yes, messy drawing! We're gonna do some gesture drawing! Watch me."

Digger picked up his Conte crayon and began to draw the main direction of Carmen's pose, the curve of her spine, in a slashing, frantic sawing motion, back and forth... He had first read about this in his bible, *How to Draw Comics the Marvel Way,* years ago.

"See the main direction of her body? That's what I've been drawing. Now, I'm gonna draw her legs! Notice, I'm not lifting my crayon from the paper. It's messy drawing!"

The kids giggled every time he said that.

"Look between the legs. There is a triangle of space there, right?"

"Right!"

"Let's draw that triangle on our paper!"

Digger likewise drew in the arms with that same scribbly, directional mess of lines.

He emphasized the angles of the hips and shoulders and showed the children how to check these angles against the angles of the model's body, by using their thumb.

Digger was thrilled with these kids, reminding himself that they had begun learning the violin and piano at age three.

"Contrapposto!" Digger yelled.

"Contrapposto!" the children echoed.

"Okay! Great job, Carmen," said Digger, dismissing the grateful woman.

"Now, Marcos. You're up."

The kids each returned to their easels and picked up their Conté crayons.

"Are you ready to do some messy drawing?"

"Yes!" they shouted.

"Alright. Marcos, could you please take this broom and pretend to sweep?"

"*Claro.*"

Marcos picked up the broom and got into position. He held that pose while Digger checked his watch.

"Okay. This'll be for two minutes... and... draw!"

Digger stood behind and between the twins. He guided them.

"Start with a stick figure! See how he bends to the side? Draw that! Draw the bend! And keep it messy!"

The children squealed as they drew frantically, following Digger's every instruction.

Marcos was starting to shake, trying to hold the pose. Digger checked his watch.

"Only one more minute, Marcos!"

"Sí señor!"

"Draw a shoebox for the head! It's tilted right? Draw a tilted shoebox!" Digger looked at his watch again. "And... time!"

Marcos broke the pose and the kids stopped their slashing at their pads, bursting into laughter.

"Time to critique! Kids, attention!"

The kids sat on their hands, waiting for whatever was next.

Digger placed their easels side by side in order to display their drawings. He pointed at Paloma's page. It was taken up entirely by an unmistakable depiction of a man sweeping.

"Paloma? I see very strong movement here." Digger used his flattened hand to mimic the angles of the drawings arms and legs. "Do you see?"

Paloma nodded, not robotically either. She understood. "Pablo?"

Pablo sat up straight.

"This feels heavy here. His body is heavy. You captured that. Do you see?"

"I think I see," answered Pablo.

Digger took a vote to see how to spend the final quarter of the hour, free drawing or continuing to draw Carmen and Marco, "messy style." The kids opted to sketch the models.

Carmen and Marcos seemed fascinated by the children and by Digger.

Digger thanked and dismissed them. They walked off, chatting up a storm with one another. Surely, this would be making its way through the house staff grapevine.

Chapter 22 - *Siesta*

Digger was taking an afternoon nap when he heard his doorknob jiggling. He raised up upon his elbows as he heard a key enter the lock and turn. He was startled but not too afraid. After all, this place seemed pretty safe. It was secluded and seemed well-protected.

The door opened. It was Maya, the staff member Digger had seen in the foyer of the main house when he'd first arrived. She bore a stack of fresh linens in a large basket.

"*Oh! Lo siento! I'm sorry!*" Maya yelped, quickly backing away.

"No, no! Maya, come back!" Digger called out.

Maya entered the cottage trepidatiously. Digger stood, rubbing the sleep from his eyes.

"I came to change your bedding and your towels," she said in Spanish. "I can come back later."

"No! Here. I'll get out of your way." Digger went over to the kitchenette and leaned on the counter. "See? No problem."

Maya didn't look completely convinced. Perhaps it was due to staff rules, perhaps due to the social custom that a young lady didn't spend time alone in a man's quarters.

Digger didn't move. Maya then set into motion, stripping the bed and replacing the sheets and the towels. Digger's stare was somewhere between sweet and predatory.

When she was finished, he went to open the door for her. She floundered.

"*Adios,*" Digger said.

"*Sí, Señor. Adios,*" Maya replied scurrying away.

A shower. That's what I need, thought Digger. *A tidy place to think about Maya.*

Chapter 23 - Experience, A Plus

In his studio, Digger was trying to sort out a problem.

The twins' first few lessons were fine, but Digger needed to have models who wore very little, and he didn't feel right asking the gardener and the chambermaid to strip down to their bathing suits. Besides, holding dynamic poses was tough stuff. He got an idea.

Digger wrote out a stack of 3x5-inch index cards, half in Spanish, half in English, reading:

WANTED:
MALE AND FEMALE HEAD AND FIGURE MODELS
FOR PRIVATE STUDY
NO NUDITY GOOD PAY ALL AGES
EXPERIENCE A PLUS
CONTACT DIGGER
867 53 09

Digger left a note on his door, telling of his plans to go into town, then hopped into the car and headed out.

He got out in bustling Madrid and soaked it in. Digger liked Madrid. *Any city is better with money.* Digger thought of Bridget, the theater girl who cut his hair back in California. She always said, *"Without money, we're just slaves."*

He first purchased an answering machine at an electronics shop. Then, he hit the colleges and universities, tacking up the cards on bulletin boards. Next were the public squares and in front of the museums.

"What's that you are putting up there?" asked a voice behind Digger. Oh, crap. He was getting busted for putting the cards up where he wasn't supposed to.

"Looking for models to make some extra money. You interested?" Digger responded without turning around. *Please don't be a cop. Please don't be a cop.*

"Yeah, sure."

Digger turned around to see a lean young man with a sparse and spotty beard and a heap of dark curls wearing a *futbol* T-shirt. He reminded Digger of his best friend Kevin, back in the States.

"Great! Let me ask you something. How in love are you with that beard?"

Chapter 24 - Jester Drawing

Digger had the new model, Leon—his name was Leon—wear or bring a pair of shorts and a tank top under his shirt. Leon had shaved off his scraggly beard, making his head and face easier for the children to draw.

Leon was cartoonish in his awe at the grandeur of the mansion. He was quite happy with the pay he was promised as well. He was a university student. He asked Digger if he did any hiking.

Digger shook his head.

"What? You are kidding!" Leon exclaimed at first sight of the children. "Them? They cannot be but five years old!"

Digger calmed Leon down and settled him into a pose, not unlike a discus thrower.

At their easels, the twins drew five five-minute poses, then two ten-minute poses before Digger gave Leon a break. He told Leon to relax, that he'd call for him when the children were ready.

Leon towelled off his sweat as he marveled at watching these attentive kids take in Digger's lecture and demo. "I had no idea that modelling could be so physically demanding!" he muttered. He'd gone through four of Digger's towels.

"Okay. Back to it." Digger had wrapped up his lecture to the twins and Leon resumed the small, square modelling stage.

When all was done, Digger told the children to thank Leon.

"*Gracias, Leon!*" they chimed.

Leon crammed his cash in his wrinkled shirt pocket and put his shoes back on.

He asked Digger again about hiking. *Oh, no,* Digger thought. *I'm not getting out of this one.*

Chapter 25 - *Toallas*

Leon had dirtied four of Digger's towels and Digger had dirtied the rest himself.

Digger picked up the phone and called housekeeping.

"*Bueno?* Could you please send Maya to bring me fresh towels? I'm all out."

Digger listened to the voice on the other end.

"*Sí.* No. That's okay," Digger responded. "I'll find her. *Gracias.*"

Digger scooped up all of his soiled towels into a big heap and carried this pile out of his cottage.

He marched across the crew-cutted grass, toward the main house.

Once inside, he encountered Carmen, who was cleaning some large windows.

"*¿Carmen, donde esta Maya?*" questioned Digger, asking Maya's whereabouts.

Carmen said that she didn't know, her eyes wide with surprise at seeing Digger carrying this heap of dirty towels.

"*No importa. Gracias!*" Digger said.

With that, Digger continued his quest.

He went to the top of a staircase, where he heard a voice from below.

"Señor Digger?" It was Gustavo.

Digger descended the stairs to meet him.

"I was informed that you are in need of some towels."

"Uh, yes."

"Here. Let me take those from you," Gustavo offered. "Now, you can go back to your apartment and I will have fresh *toallas* brought to you,"

Digger felt reprimanded by Gustavo's perpetual smile. He thanked Gustavo and headed back to his quarters.

*

Digger put on a pair of shorts and a T-shirt. A jog sounded good. He had some kinks to get out. He opened the door to leave his place and startled both himself and Maya, who was standing there, bearing a stack of fresh towels.

"Please, come in," said Digger in Spanish.

"*Toallas frescas*, Fresh towels," said Maya, raising her load for emphasis.

She dutifully replaced the missing towels in the bathroom, as well as the extras he had requested for the model for the children's next art lesson.

Digger fidgeted. He didn't want her to leave, but knew she would, just as soon as she had completed her task. He wanted to make conversation, but knew that would be too transparent.

No, he didn't want her to go... and, she didn't.

Maya stood there silent. She couldn't have been waiting for dismissal. She had practically knocked the door down, trying to get out the last time she was there.

No. She was staying put. It couldn't have been her idea. Did Gustavo tell her to stay?

Digger's head spun.

He invited her to sit and she did. She didn't look meek, though.

He found Maya unbelievably appealing but was she here as some sort of offering or did her earlier eye contact mean that she was attracted to him also? The predator in him rejoiced while his better angel told him to cool his jets.

He stood and held the door for Maya, thanking her for the *toallas*.

She nodded and walked out. She took a few steps before she looked back upon him and gave Digger a tiny smile.

Chapter 26 - I Guess That's to be Expected

Francesca brought the children in from playing to take them to their art lessons.

That way was best. That way the kids burned off some energy and were less hyperactive and more attentive. They really were wonderful children… bright, attentive, respectful, affectionate and confident. They were simply beautiful, to boot.

Álvaro. What a surprise he was in her life, much older, very wise, handsome, wealthy yet truly unattached to material things. He was a terrific lover, a lover of life, a lover of family. And, he had given her these miracle children.

Francesca thought that she had been doomed to spinsterhood after a dumb and devastating divorce, earlier in life. She had been young, but that was no excuse. She had been warned, warned by *everybody*. *Don't do it*, they'd said, but she had been walking blindfolded with her fingers in her ears.

Ah, but that was in another life. Now, these children were her life—she had no others—and it was time for art lessons.

Today, the children were painting a woman in a large and elaborate skirt with a large hat and parasol. Digger had been quite creative with the children. They loved him.

The woman was in her early twenties and looked like an old, turn-of-the-century advertisement for Coca-Cola.

Digger had the children drawing and painting models of all shapes, ages and sizes. Always costumed. Never nude. It was a stroke of genius for Álvaro to hire him for the twins' education.

She had thought for a while that he had a little crush on her, but that seemed to have subsided, which was good for her husband was an understanding man, to a point.

Digger had them painting in acrylics. Unlike oils, acrylics dried nearly instantly. This taught the children to make quick decisions, to not rely on fussy blending, according to Digger.

He showed up and Pablo rushed him for a hug. Paloma copied this action.

Digger showed the models tremendous courtesy, offering them beverages and the use of electric fans if they got too warm in their costumes, as well as heaters if they grew too cold.

He set all in place and got the children started. He guided them through choosing where they were to place the figure on the drawing or painting surface. Sometimes, they painted on paper, sometimes on canvas board and other times on stretched canvas. Francesca loved to watch the kids gesso their blank canvases. They looked so focused, so accomplished, so professional.

Francesca wandered behind Digger as he monitored the children's progress.

A sketchbook lay on the table. She picked it up. She flipped to the back to see the most recent entries first. Her heart swelled when she saw the head studies, little portraits of her own little angels, Pablo and Paloma in there. The quick sketches belonged on a cathedral wall, so precious were they.

She flipped through a few more pages and her heart returned to its normal size. In fact, it raced just a bit. Images of flayed bodies filled the pages. This made sense. Many artists studied anatomy and showed the human figure in different states of dismemberment, but when the images showed more situations suitable for the Spanish Inquisition, she was given pause. These sketches of torture devices and scenarii were drawn with no sort of academic detachment. They were indulging something, something living, something dark.

Francesca's mind raced. Such places this young man's mind went. But, look at him, so good with the children. Her own husband had his secrets and she accepted them wholly.

Skinny Digger had charisma. Good people and bad could have charisma.

Right before she was set to close the book, she saw them.

There were sketches of her, pages of them. Many from memory, but one distinctly taken from an old photograph of her, smiling confidently. Mild shock ran through her bones. She looked up at Digger, teaching the children, and just stood there, waiting for this shock to wear off. It finally did.

So long as she kept an eye on skinny Digger and the kids continued to blossom under his tutelage, she chose to embrace him. And she assured herself that if the day came that he was no longer good for them, she had only to let her husband know, for she married a very resourceful man.

Francesca slammed the book shut and placed it back on the table, unnoticed by anybody, save the woman who was sweating in the sun under a hat that hurt more than it helped.

Chapter 27 - Hiking

"I don't have a car," Leon confessed on the telephone. "Could you pick me up?"

Thirty minutes later, Digger pulled up to the hostel, where Leon was not waiting outside as planned.

After waiting in the car for ten minutes, Digger turned off the car and entered.

He found Leon and his shocks of curls sitting on a bunk, surrounded by laughing students. An unplayed guitar lay on one of the beds.

"Ah, here he is!" announced Leon to the room.

Digger had learned that Spaniard punctuality was somewhat elastic, but he was still a little irritated with Leon's lack of readiness.

"Ready to go, Leon?" asked Digger, feigning a neutrality of demeanor.

"Digger! Let me introduce you! This is Pauline…"

Digger nodded and exchanged names with the room's inhabitants, wishing to get a move on. After a while though, his attitude softened and he gave in to enjoying the moment.

The character of the rustling scene reminded Digger of a locker room pre-game huddle.

Leon invited some of his bunkmates along on their hiking trip, which Digger felt presumptuous. But, alas, they all had other plans.

Digger and Leon drove out of central Madrid and toward the trailhead.

He parked the car and they exited. Digger locked it, not knowing why. Perhaps, out of sheer force of habit. There were no valuables in it, but if someone wanted to steal the car and knew how to hot wire it, they certainly knew how to open a locked car door. The trailhead was half packed with rental cars as well as those of local ownership.

For just a moment, Digger had the idea that Leon might be some kind of decoy and that this was all a plan to rob him or steal the car.

They hit the trail.

With his non-stop and aimless chatter, Leon got on Digger's nerves at first, but then they broke into patches of silence, punctuated by ever more enjoyable snatches of conversation. Leon did most of the talking, telling Digger the bulk of his life's story and recent exploits.

The trail was wide and well-worn with tall grass on either side.

They passed farms and vineyards in the distance.

Leon found a large branch for Digger to use as a hiking stick.

They reached an upgrade that became a nuisance, then a trial for Digger.

"Look straight down," instructed Leon. "Keep telling yourself, *the ground is flat. The ground is flat.*" The trick seemed to work to Digger's surprise.

Leon had brought a water canteen and some trail mix made of sunflower seeds and dried blueberries in his daypack.

After hours of hiking, Digger realized that the sneakers he wore were no substitute for real hiking shoes. He was getting blisters on his feet. Why did he agree to this?

The position of the sun, as well as Digger's own fatigue, told him to suggest heading back.

"You wouldn't mind if I kept hiking solo, would you?" asked Leon. "I could catch a ride into town from the trailhead, then take public transport or walk from there to the hostel."

It was an odd request Digger thought, but not an unwelcome one.

Digger told him he'd call about more modelling work. Leon thanked Digger for his company and for joining him on the hike. He waved goodbye and ventured forth, while Digger turned back.

Digger nodded and exchanged greetings with hikers travelling in the opposite direction. He saw a couple of attractive young women that elicited some grizzly thoughts, thoughts that involved teeth, thoughts that involved rope. He told himself again that he was not the author of these thoughts. He closed his eyes and allowed these thoughts to swim by him like a school of fish.

Digger saw some fellow travellers sitting on a stone wall and joined them. The vista around him was lovely. The sun was beginning to hang low, so Digger headed for the car.

The car was gone.

Frantically, Digger searched all around. There were a few different parking areas. Could he have merely misremembered which he had used? Had he been duped by Leon and his hostel mates?

Just then, he saw a group of American college students playing a prank. Six of them were lifting a small convertible sportscar and moving it under a large nearby tree.

Was this what happened? Did a bunch of knuckleheaded pranksters merely move his car?

Digger continued to search until he found it, right where he had parked it, in a lot identical to the others, but farther away.

He drove back to the house, oh, so grateful to still have the Porsche in one piece. He had no idea what he would have told Álvaro if he hadn't. Sure, the expense would likely not break a man of such wealth, but the humiliation and embarrassment would have been unbearable, not to mention the complete loss of credibility.

Digger was hungry. He might call the kitchen and ask for a sandwich. *Nah, I've got enough food in the fridge.* He grazed on Jamón Ibérico, grapes and crusty bread.

Digger was glad to be "home." He would have time to get some studying done and to work on his new secret project.

Books of John Singer Sargent, Diego Velázquez and Caravaggio were splayed all over the worktable in Digger's studio. He wore his painting jeans and no shirt as he placed the 2x4 ft. canvas onto his easel. A leftover tape played from the boom box.

Digger opened all of the windows and turned on a couple of electric fans for maximum ventilation. The cold kept him sharp, he told himself.

He opened his current sketchbook and flipped through its pages until he landed upon those that began the studies of Paloma and Pablo.

Their five-year-old faces were born to be painted. He would present this double-portrait to the family upon its completion, as a gesture of affection and gratitude, gratitude for their hospitality, their generosity and for this adventure.

He chose a few angles of the faces that he would combine. Next, he blocked out a simple and basic composition on the canvas, using a Conté crayon, improvising the pose. Digger then refined each line, the contours of the shoulders, the outline of the stiff shirts that he invented. His sketches only had their heads defined, not any clothing.

Digger mixed up a thin mixture of paint and turps with a one-inch brush in a jar.

He now stood, staring at his handiwork, the Conté "underdrawing" that was to be the foundation of his painting, his portrait.

Digger enjoyed his own work. Sure, he knew that he had eons of learning ahead of him, but he was good enough to please himself. He also had a pretty good idea of exactly how good he was. After all, false modesty was just that, false. A lie.

He steeled himself, as if on a high-diving board, then took a three-inch flat brush and lightly covered the entire canvas, fixing the drawing to it and knocking the whole thing back from gesso white to a medium-dark sepia tone. He worked carefully not to smear or smudge the underdrawing.

Digger took out a rag and began to scrub out some light areas with his finger—the light shirts, the children's cheeks, highlights of the hair…

He squeezed out some oil paint onto his palette. He would work in a Zorn palette, limiting his color range to give the portrait an Old World feel.

Digger grabbed a palette knife and began to mix his colors, thereby launching his plan to keep them young forever.

Chapter 28 - Churros y Chocolate

Digger saw a *churro y chocolate* shop just off the Gran Via in Madrid.

Mmmm. Churros.

He saw two lines of patrons standing and opted to stand in the shorter line, the one that had a sign reading, *"Para Llevar."* Digger remarked to himself that the Spanish always seemed so well-dressed. No sweatshirts, save for those trying to look like Americans. They certainly had an influence upon him. He was dressing and feeling more stylish every day.

When he reached the front of the line, Digger ordered his *churros con chocolate* and left the counter. As he was leaving the store, he noticed all of the outdoor café tables and chose one to sit and enjoy his treat.

Mmmm, this was good. Dunking the long, fried donut-like delicacies, rolled in sugar-cinnamon into the thick and rich chocolate, was as delicious a sin as any.

Just then, a man in an apron with the store logo came upon Digger and scolded him, wagging his entire hand. He could not sit here! These tables were for those who waited in the longer, *Para Aqui*, "For Here" line!

Embarrassed and fumbling, Digger made quick work of leaving the table and taking his snack on the go.

He was making his way down the street when suddenly, he and the pickpocket brother of the man Digger had killed spotted each other, to each other's utter shock.

The man broke into a sprint toward Digger and Digger bolted from him instantly, dropping his churros and chocolate.

He chased Digger through streets and across plazas, through courtyards and down alleys. Digger had youth on his side, but the man knew these cities like he knew his own house and he caught Digger by heading him off. Digger ran right into him when the man emerged from around the corner.

It was crowded but the man did not seem to care. He whipped out a switchblade that glistened in the light. His smile was not of delight, but of wrath.

Digger turned around to run, knocking over a small group of locals like bowling pins.

Others grabbed and held Digger until the police could be summoned. This was *not* like Andalusia.

The man got away. Digger went to jail.

The police were not as friendly as the ones who just slapped Digger on the back and sent him on his merry way. No, these guys meant business. Here, being an American tourist seemed a bigger liability than an asset.

The police interrogated him and he talked about being attacked by a pickpocket.

They showed him a book of mugshots. Digger identified the man. The name under the photo read, "Daniel."

The two cops looked at each other. They must have known Daniel.

Digger believed that he would rot there, until he had the idea to have the police call Álvaro. Within an hour, Sonia the lawyer showed up and bailed him out.

"So, you're a criminal lawyer?" asked Digger as they left the building.

"Contract law, probate, criminal, whatever Señor Téllez needs me to do for him."

"Do you do that for all of your clients?"

"Señor Téllez is my only client."

*

Later in the day, Gustavo summoned Digger and led him to see Álvaro in his study, three staircases down into the cool earth below the main house.

A refrigerator-chested security man stood next to Álvaro, who sat at a grand wooden desk. Next to Refrigerator Man, on the opposite side, was Daniel, who launched out of his seat at the sight of Digger before Refrigerator's large hand planted him right back down.

"Digger. This is the man who attacked you?" asked Álvaro.

"That little *puto* killed *mi hermano*," spat Daniel.

"Who attacked my daughter, yes?"

"Her purse is not worth his life!"

Álvaro seemed to ignore the man's challenge to the equivalence.

"Digger, do you wish me to kill this man?"

Digger was in a tight spot. He didn't know who he was really dealing with here. Sure, having the guy dead would mean not looking over his shoulder all of the time, but what kind of strings would that place on him with Álvaro? He had the distinct impression that he was getting in way over his head.

"I do, but no. No, I don't," Digger finally answered.

"Jordi, get rid of him. I can't have him running around the streets, looking to kill one of my men."

With great force Daniel again tried to heave himself out of his chair but was again stopped by the large, square Jordi.

"No. Don't," pleaded Digger half-heartedly.

"Please. Consider it a gift, a mere token of my gratitude. My children just love you."

*

Later, it weighed on Digger that Álvaro had the means and mind to order a death so casually, not so much as a moral issue, but one of self-preservation. Digger did not wish to walk on eggshells for a man who could rub him out if he grew tired of him.

"One of *my men*," Álvaro had said. Digger didn't feel those words carried as much a sense of association as they did of possession.

This heightened feeling lessened over time, although the lesson did not. Digger now knew to be careful, very careful.

Chapter 29 - Painting Each Other

Digger brought the boom box from his apartment so that the children could have some music while they worked today. They had been painting each other, doing studies in preparation for Christmas portraits they would give to their parents on El Día de Reyes Magos, a few weeks from then.

At the children's spirited request, he tuned the radio to a local station that played pop hits from Europe and the Americas until it got them too hyperactive. They kept bopping in their seats to the music. When it affected their focus, Digger changed the station to classical. That was more like it.

Digger circled the two five-year-old masters as they blocked in and carved out shapes, shapes of hair, shapes of shirt sleeves... They were getting remarkably good.

They squinted and pulled back their heads. They raised their thumbs and measured.

Some of the staff gathered to gaze briefly at what their little charges were creating. They gasped when they saw what was coming out of these five-year-olds. It showed them what came of growing up with money.

Nodding approvingly, the staff members left and got back to their duties.

Pablo broke the twins' silence.

"We love you, Digger."

Paloma nodded like her spring broke.

"Hold still, Paloma. I'm working on your nose," said Pablo.

Chapter 30 - El Gordo

It was officially the Spanish Christmas season. The house was decorated with strings of lights, multiple Christmas trees, nativity scenes and food, lots of food.

The twins, Paloma and Pablo, wiggled in place, seated on the floor in front of the 60-inch, rear-projection TV in their pajamas. The relatively small—well, small for a mansion—TV room was cozy. Álvaro and Francesca sat in their respective highback chairs. Digger sat at the end of a sofa.

It was December 22nd, the day of the El Gordo lottery, the oldest lottery in the world. Three-quarters of the country of Spain played it. The twins had tickets. Gustavo had taken care of that. They held their tickets in their tight little fists.

"What are you going to do if they were to win? It would be obscene," said Francesca, working on some elaborate needlework.

"They are not going to win, Francesca."

"And what if they did? We would have to give that money to the poor!"

"Let them have their fun, Francesca."

This was something of a Christmas tradition, so they invited Digger to come, probably thinking that he would decline, but Digger found the whole thing fascinating. Well, if not fascinating, very interesting.

When Pablo looked at Digger, Digger made a face of cartoonish excitement, shaking his fists wildly. This made Pablo squeal. Paloma was listing all of the things she wanted aloud, another donkey, a castle like a princess, but with a dungeon and another donkey.

On TV, there were two giant gold globes, one larger, one smaller, filled with golden balls.

A procession of singing children came out wearing uniforms and marched across the stage.

Later, two of the singing children were chosen to pick out the balls with the winning lottery numbers.

Each winning number made the twins flip out. They jumped and danced around, probably also owing to the amount of pure holiday sugar rushing through their veins.

A uniformed servant brought in a tray of hot chocolate for all.

"So, tell us, Digger. How do you celebrate Christmas with your family in the United States?" asked Álvaro.

"We buy stuff and return it to the store because it wasn't what we wanted."

Álvaro didn't pursue this line of questioning.

They all sipped their hot chocolates and watched the children watch the TV.

The twins were stretching to new heights every day. Digger couldn't help but feel something close to pride when he looked at them.

*

After Digger's father had left his mother with two small children to raise, Christmas became something of a nomadic affair. They spent the day with upper-class friends of the family. Digger always had the feeling that there was a measure of pity that marbled the invitation.

He and his sister Audrey would each receive a mercy gift from the hosts and then watch their hosts' ungrateful children tear into their unlimited presents.

The couple of Christmases Digger *did* remember spending at home were magical. They were low-key and mellow: "Christmas with the Chipmunks" spun on the family stereo, candy from a store-bought stocking and plenty of modest gifts, lots to open. Silly String, a Rocky and Bullwinkle sleeping bag and a toy robot from a faraway aunt.

Despite all of that, Digger simply *adored* Christmas: the lights, the food, the music, the caroling and, yes, the presents, although, as he got older he found that the real action was in the giving of gifts. Receiving a gift was a short-lived thrill, nothing next to the weeks or months of anticipation in the hunting, perusing and choosing, the hiding and wrapping. Yes, Digger loved giving gifts. Just ask Beverly.

Chapter 31 - Mass

In his private apartment, Digger was flipping through an El Corte Inglés shopping catalog, agonizing over what to get the twins for Christmas. Luckily, in Spain, the major gift giving came in about a week and a half during El Día de Reyes Magos, so he still had a little time to figure something out, as it was only Christmas Eve.

He checked his watch—time to get a move on.

Digger headed up to the main house on foot. It was cold, surprisingly colder than Los Angeles in the wintertime. His ears and nose started to lose feeling as he finally neared the mansion.

He entered through a side door and made his way to the grand dining room.

He was the first one there. Digger went through his options and settled on just standing there until somebody else showed up.

The empty room was predictably large, with a long dining table and chandeliers. All of the chairs led him to believe that there would be more guests than just the immediate family.

Just then, people began to file into the room.

Maria Lucia and Basilio were in attendance, each with a date. They would all be staying for only a few days. They would come back, however, for El Día de Reyes Magos. There were cousins, aunts and uncles.

Tonight was the *Nochebuena* dinner, the Christmas Eve feast, during which the meal centered around turkey and *turrón* nougat candy. The smell of it made Digger salivate.

Digger felt bad about the servants who worked the holidays. They most likely had families too.

The meal was lovely, punctuated with laughter and song. Well-behaved children were hoisted into the air.

After eating, the family piled into the cars and caravanned into town, where they took a walk on the Gran Via, with all the lights and *Nacimientos* (Nativity scenes), but no *Misa del Gallo* (mass).

"No mass?" asked Digger, genuinely surprised as he thought of Spain as a devout Catholic country.

"No *mas*!" joked Ávalo.

After a bit, the children began to fade, so they all came back to the main house.

"I'm going to cut out and go to mass," Basilio told Digger into his ear.

"Mass? But I thought—"

"Not for the religiosity, but for the cultural grandeur. You should come. It is quite beautiful. My father, he gave you my old car, yes?" asked Basilio.

"Yes," Digger answered, a tad embarrassed. "On loan," he quickly added, hoping to soften how it sounded.

"Good. We'll take it."

"What about your date?" asked Digger.

"She is tired and wants to get some rest. Besides, she does not care much for religious spectacle," responded Basilio.

*

Digger drove them from the main house onto the public street. Basilio pulled the glove compartment open. "Oh, good. It is still here." He pulled out a cassette and pushed it into the tape deck. John Cale's *Paris 1919* album began to play.

"Oh!" exclaimed Basilio, enraptured by the sound. "Do you know this? Do you know John Cale?"

"From The Velvet Underground, right? Lou Reed?"

"Lou Reed," Basilio spat. "Lou Reed couldn't shine John Cale's shoes."

Basilio looked at the Porsche's quartz clock.

"We are going to be early. That's good. It's good to be at least an hour early."

"How early are we?"

"Two hours."

After parking the car, they walked Calle Mayor to the Catedral de Santa María la Real de la Almudena for mass. The crypt was closed. All tourism was closed during mass.

While they stood in line, Basilio was surprisingly quiet. The few times that Digger initiated conversation, Basilio would lower his eyelids, his hands clasped in front of him.

Finally, they were let in. Digger could hear the organ music as they passed between and under the columns, sculptures, and bas-relief plaques.

Once inside, the procession moved past more columns and mosaics, the painting-like pictures made purely of thousands of thousands of small tiles. These tiles reminded Digger of Diego Velásquez, who, unlike most of the painters of his day, did not employ much blending of paint colors. He would paint tile-like shapes next to each other, so perfectly mixed that the eye thought it was looking at gradations of color caused by blending. It was just like these mosaics.

Grand organ music pumped overhead, holding up the cathedral's infinite ceiling.

Basilio whispered in Digger's ear.

"La Banda Sinfónica Municipal de Madrid holds concerts here, for Easter… not mass, though."

The mass lasted between ninety minutes and a couple of hours.

Basilio spotted some attractive young ladies as he and Digger were leaving the *catedral*. They may have been prostitutes. He tried to convince Digger that they should go talk to them, ask them to join them in some nighttime activities, but Digger killed his buzz. They walked around the outside of the cathedral. It was impressive, lit up at night like this.

"What do you have that's like this where you live, Digger?"

Digger blew his lips out, trying to come up with an answer.

"Well," he began, buying for time, "I guess there is the Griffith Park Observatory."

"An observatory? That sounds fascinating."

"Yeah. I guess. They filmed 'Rebel Without a Cause' there. It's all Art Deco." Digger wracked his brain. "And, there's the Hollywood Walk of Fame."

"That's where the winos piss on the movie stars?"

"Yeah, that's it."

Digger felt like heading back home although Basilio had hinted at more prowling. They wound up heading back. After all, it was Christmas.

The days following were as lazy as imaginable. Digger didn't seem to be missed as he hibernated, snacked, read and watched holiday specials on TV. The children were on holiday, so no art classes. He was left to his own devices, which meant a significant amount of aimless driving at night and walking during the day. Digger went gift shopping with purpose but without panic.

Chapter 32 - The Face of a Walnut

Two slender kidnappers slithered through the parade crowd. One a tad taller. He wore a Pendleton cap. The shorter man had the face of a walnut. They found a good spot and stopped for a while, but not to watch the parade.

Chapter 33 - I Love a Parade

Francesca and a housemaid were wriggling the twins into their winter clothing. This year was particularly cold and she thought it best to put the kids in their fur coats for *La Cabalgata de Reyes Magos*, the Parade of the Three Kings, where they celebrate the coming of the Three Wise Men.

She brought the children downstairs where their father greeted them excitedly.

"*Mis hijos!*" he exclaimed, embracing the children who ran into him soundly.

"*Andiamo alla parata, papá?*"

"Paloma! You know I don't speak Italian!" Álvaro said in cheerful Spanish.

"She wants to know if we are going to the parade!" translated Pablo.

Maria Lucia, Basilio and Digger all congregated in the grand foyer of the main house.

"The driver is here for whenever you are ready," Gustavo informed his boss Álvaro.

They all piled into the limousine, Digger entering last.

"*Cómo estás*, Everett?" Álvaro asked the driver, surprising Digger. Everett was not a Spanish name.

"Splendid, *Señor! Y usted?*" answered Everett in a dialect as crisp as a potato chip.

On the way, the children led the carload in singing *villancicos*, Christmas songs, with great gusto. Digger clapped and sang along, as the songs were simple and easy to join in.

They arrived at a specified drop-off point and all disembarked from the large town car.

All wedged their way together through the crowd toward their ideal vantage point, finally settling in front of a large department store.

Pablo rode Basilio's shoulders, while Paloma stayed put on the ground, firmly grasping her mother Francesca's hand. Maria Lucia and Digger did little bounces in place, trying to keep warm.

The children were bundled up to their faces in their fur coats. Francesca wore one as well. Álvaro, Maria Lucia, Basilio and Digger wore lighter jackets.

Not only were the children getting antsy, waiting for the parade to begin, the entire crowd throbbed and bobbed, rubbing their mittens together to keep warm.

At last, they heard whistles and the loud bang of fireworks, igniting the crowd into cheers and the spontaneous appearance of confetti from poppers in the crowd.

A pack of live camels passed by, jockeyed by men in glittering turbans, followed by a troupe of men on stilts performing stunts and acrobatics.

The children shrieked and applauded as marching bands played, passing by in near-military precision. There were bicycles and a fire truck that tooted its horn.

The whole family waved to the floats and horses.

Francesca applauded with great *fuerza* until she realized that she no longer held onto Paloma's hand. She looked down. Where was Paloma?

She looked all around her and the little girl was not to be seen. Francesca began to panic.

"Álvaro? Can you see Paloma? I can't see her!" she shouted above the crowd.

Immediately, Basilio, Digger and Maria Lucia heard this and their attention dropped from the parade. They began to scour around their own knees, then widened their gaze outward around them.

"Paloma!" each shouted, pushing through the crowd.

"We meet right back here!" shouted Basilio as he darted around the crowd like a shark.

Terrified, Digger pushed his way through the crowd. It was like looking for something underwater. She could be anywhere.

"¿Miraste una chica morena bajita, como cinco años?" Digger asked person after person, sometimes shoving, sometimes grasping lapels. He looked left and right, jumping in place in order to see over the crowd. He could hear Francesca sobbing loudly over the din.

Just then, Digger caught glimpse of Paloma. She was being yanked away by the arm by two men, one wearing a Pendleton cap.

Digger yelled, "I see her!" and gave chase.

The man without the cap scooped her up and carried her. Paloma was paralyzed with terror.

They dragged her away from the crowd and down a side street, disappearing from Digger's view.

Digger ran after them, yelling, "Basilio!" the whole way. He ran past and alley, then skidded to a halt and doubled back.

He saw them in a more secluded area, in the shadows of the alley.

When Digger yelled her name, the men stopped and faced him.

"If you want her back, you will give us money," the man in the cap said.

"Yes. Yes, I have money," Digger panted.

"Come with us to the *cajero*. You will give us money and we will give you the girl."

Brave little Paloma was wide eyed with panic, but did not scream.

Digger followed them to the *cajero*, the ATM. He stood at the keypad while the two kidnappers stood farther away. Paloma, now restrained by a fist gripping her fur-lined collar, stood between the two criminals. she was shaking with more than cold.

"How much do you want?" asked Digger, trying not to sound combative.

"Take out all you can, plus, whatever you have in your wallet."

"Fine. Fine."

Just then, Digger saw right behind them, a looming figure.

It was Basilio. He front-kicked the man who had Paloma in the small of the back, causing the man to release her. Digger wasn't certain that Basilio hadn't broken the man's pelvis.

Digger lunged forward toward the other abductor but the man pulled a gun on him. Basilio grabbed him about the waist as the man in the cap writhed in agony on the ground.

Paloma ran, disappearing around a corner.

The gun went off, catching Digger in the thigh.

Paloma ran into Maria Lucia.

Basilio wrestled the gun from the assailant and held it under his chin.

"You have really made a mess of your life," he said in Spanish.

The man grit his teeth, not giving Basilio the satisfaction of a response.

"Your short, short life."

Digger was taken to the hospital by ambulance. His teeth remained clenched in pain.

"Were the police called?" Digger asked Basilio, on the ride to the hospital.

"They will be dealt with."

*

Digger arrived at a private hospital for the, apparently, rich and connected. There was no waiting. He was rushed right in.

Dr. Gascon removed the bullet from the fleshy part of Digger's thigh with a local anesthetic.

"Ah, we are lucky today. Missed the femur as well as the femoral artery. It is a little deep, but it is still just a flesh wound," said Dr. Gascon in his elevated Spanish.

"How will this affect his walking?" asked a concerned Basilio.

By now, Digger's Spanish was fluent. His apprehension was solid as was his pronunciation. He understood every word.

"You," Dr. Gascon spoke directly to Digger, "Will limp, will require a cane to walk for a little bit. I'd say a couple of months at the very most. I will give you something for the pain."

"I take it you are close to the Téllez family?" asked Digger.

"I delivered the twins, as well as Maria Lucia and Basilio," began Dr. Gascon with less humor than Digger would've expected. "So, yes, I would say that I am close to the family. Now, if you'll excuse me, I have a matter to attend to." He turned to Basilio.

"Basilio, tell your father that I will be right with him."

Digger's imagination reeled. The doctor had been called in. He wasn't serendipitously doing rounds at the hospital. Granted, this was a private hospital, but what would the doctor have to discuss with Álvaro? Surely, it wasn't billing. Did Álvaro have a secret condition the doctor was monitoring?

No, there was something about the doctor's demeanor that led Digger to believe that his matter with Álvaro had to do with the kidnapper. Perhaps Dr. Gascon was to be Álvaro's dealer of justice. No. Too much imagination, Digger thought.

Digger remained in the hospital overnight, just in case.

When he awoke in the middle of the night to use the restroom, stubborn Digger did not hit the call button for assistance as ordered. He groaned and strained as he attempted to swing his legs to the side of the bed. It took a few tries, but he was able to reach the crutches that leaned against the chair next to the bed.

The strain and pain of walking caused sweat to trickle down Digger's back.

Hobbling back from the toilet, Digger noticed, outside the open door to his room, the refrigerator-shaped Jordi, standing guard. Digger did not attempt communication.

Chapter 34 - The Thrill is Gone

That morning, the morning of El Día de Los Reyes Magos, the staff had already taken down the Christmas trees and most of the decorations, as is the custom.

The twins came down the stairs, but not with the boundless energy and excitement befitting the holiday. They were somber as they descended upon their glistening piles of gifts.

Francesca refrained from asking the children what was wrong, for she knew well what was wrong with them. It was the very same thing that was wrong with her, that was wrong with her husband Álvaro.

Two armed men had kidnapped their beloved daughter Paloma the previous night and held her for ransom. She was saved by Digger and Paloma's half brother Basilio.

Francesca knew that it was insane, but she couldn't help but resent Digger for all of this. Maybe it was just easiest to blame Digger. After all, it was Francesca who had lost track of the little girl, dropped her hand at the parade and had not noticed her absence until the child had completely disappeared into the vast and bustling parade crowd.

Álvaro entered the room, carrying the last of the gifts.

Digger was still in the hospital.

"This might be a good thing, Digger staying in the hospital for a little bit." Álvaro whispered to his wife. "This is all too fresh. Digger saved our daughter's life. I know that.

But, right now, it's probably best to keep her away from any reminders of last night."

The children ate their sweet holiday treats, zombie-eyed.

They began to open their gifts. They were mostly silly, small trinkets and toys. As wealthy as the family was, Álvaro did not want his children to become slaves to material possessions. They got chocolates, small toy cars and stuffed animals.

Francesca picked up a pair of identically wrapped presents, addressed to each of the children.

"Here, *bambini*," she said delicately. "They're from Digger."

Pablo stared at his gift for a moment. He then began to unwrap it slowly.

It was a leather-bound sketchbook, fastened by a thin belt. He undid the belt and opened the book. It was inscribed in Spanish.

Pablo, you are a true artist! With affection, Digger.

Paloma just sat there staring at the brother's gift. She then looked up at her brother and got up. She took the stairs, two at a time, back to her bedroom.

Francesca looked to Álvaro, who continued to stare at his little boy.

*

Later in the day, servants brought the El Roscón de Reyes cake, Polvorones, Mantecados y mazapán candied treats to the long and elaborate holiday table for the main meal of the day.

Digger was there. He showed up on brand new aluminum crutches. "Merry Christmas, everyone!" he greeted. "It's me, Tiny Tim!"

However festive and elegant the decor, the meal itself was grim.

Digger didn't want Francesca, or anybody for that matter, to blame themselves.

"Kids break off all of the time," he reasoned. "They run off. The important thing is that Paloma is now home, safe and sound with her loving family."

The twins each ate a candy, with dead eyes.

The situation broke Digger's heart. The kids were clearly traumatized.

"Did you get my presents?" Digger asked the twins.

"Digger. Happy Día de Reyes Magos. We are fortunate that you were here when our daughter was taken," said Francesca, stiffly.

It was clear. Digger was a reminder of last night, of the kidnapping, not of all the time he spent teaching the children and falling in love with them. He would probably always be.

Álvaro cleared his throat. He began to speak again but Digger interrupted him.

"I have really enjoyed your hospitality and generosity, but I think it's time that I went back to the United States. I've loved Spain, but it's time I went home." Digger put on a fake half-smile.

The twins had complex reactions. Each had their own associations with Digger to the trauma, but they didn't want him to go, either. They began to cry at the dinner table. Pablo hopped off his chair and ran to Digger who gave him a long hug. Paloma just sat there, paralyzed.

Francesca looked relieved, which made Digger feel somehow betrayed, but he figured, that's the way things went.

Chapter 35 - Digger's Ghost

Digger was gone.

Gustavo oversaw the clearing out of his apartment. Digger took very little with him when he left. In the studio, Gustavo discovered, sitting on an easel, the most arresting portrait. It was of Paloma and Pablo, the little twins. It appeared incomplete. The garments and hair were still just blocked in. He gazed at it for a few moments. It was clearly a work of tremendous affection and mastery.

He had it boxed up and put into storage.

Chapter 36 - Sleeping on Trains

Digger took a taxi from the mansion to the train station, leaving much of what he had acquired back at his recently vacated apartment. He left the paintings, books and materials, hoping the children would eventually find use for them, although he knew they would likely be tossed out while the cottage and studio were scrubbed out for a new guest or resident.

The train station was magnificent. Digger hadn't the foggiest idea of a plan, so he opted for the one-month Eurail pass. Through his window, he watched Madrid shrink from skyscraper buildings to apartment buildings to trees and eventually to the countryside.

Still hobbling on crutches from the gunshot wound, Digger thought he'd get a temporary apartment in Paris and do some recovering.

He found an abandoned paperback copy of *Conversations with Capote* on the seat across from his. He read it until he fell asleep. Digger had no concern for his expenses. His bank accounts were so stuffed, he couldn't bear to look at the dizzying balances.

When he awoke, he met Karl, a German architecture student. He and Karl hit it off in grand style. Karl loved The Beatles and the Ramones. Karl was on his way back home. A girl with a backpack joined them for a few stops, then she got off.

Digger and Karl sang Trio songs. "Uh huh, uh huh, uh huuhhh!" They made jokes and made silly plans for Karl to visit Digger in the States. When they exchanged information, Digger gave him the wrong name.

Digger got off in France and spent a few months, some with a lover. They cooked, saw movies and walked the Seine. When he could walk again without the crutches, Digger got a temporary job working in a kitchen at a restaurant.

Then, it was on to Italy. Rome. La Dolce Vita. The famous fountain. Hangin' out on the steps. Next was Germany, then Czechoslovakia, eventually landing in Prague where he enjoyed café life until he felt the need to return to the United States.

Living in Europe, it all made sense until it didn't.

It was time to go home.

Part II - The States

Chapter 37- Back on American Soil

Digger had his hands up. The uniformed man circled him, waving a wand that squealed whenever it encountered metal. There was something rougher, coarser, less stylish about the treatment in American airports, compared to those in say, Spain or Czechoslovakia. The airport was loud and slightly triggering. He flinched at each electronic shriek and beep. He felt more raw, more naked, more vulnerable than in Europe.

Going through customs, he was asked if he had anything to declare. Digger resisted making the old Oscar Wilde joke, "Nothing but my genius."

It was now 1988 and Digger made his way toward the luggage carousel without haste. He had nowhere to be and nobody waiting for him there. Usually, that was the way he preferred it, but not this time.

He looked around, scanning the terminal, as if hoping, *just hoping* he would bump into somebody he knew, the way he did his childhood schoolmate Perry at that Andalusian nightclub. Digger was lonely.

After locating his luggage, he grabbed an LA Weekly, a Pennysaver and three newspapers from the newsstand, then took a cab from LAX. Digger always seemed to have more luggage than he'd have liked, although he packed a lean bag.

"Okay, boss," Digger asked the cabbie, "Take me to a hotel."

"Which one?"

"I don't care."

Digger missed Kevin, his childhood best friend. He missed the gang at the old Design Center drawing workshop. He also missed Beverly. Hell, he even thought about calling his abusive mother and apathetic sister Audrey. He could just pick up the phone, but... no. That was a lifetime ago. He wasn't the same Digger anymore. Those people were his old world, even if they travelled the same patch of land he now did. The thought of this made him a bit melancholy.

The world that whooshed by outside the taxi window was one of concrete, billboards and smog. It was not Mount Rushmore, nor the Statue of Liberty. No. This was Digger's America—one of strip bars and donut shops, burger stands and bus stops.

He checked into a Holiday Inn and spent the next couple of days sleeping, lounging by the pool and catching up on American television.

There was an old black and white Fred Astaire/Ginger Rogers movie on. The sweeping sets, tailored costumes and unbelievable dancing made Digger just shake his head in amazement. Astaire was, without argument, the Mozart of movement, but Digger found him creepy as an actor. He much preferred Rogers.

Although room service was available, he often took his meals in the restaurant, in order to steep in the anonymous company of his fellow travellers.

On the third day, Digger took a cab to a VW dealership where he bought a clean, used and warrantied, one-year-old white Cabriolet and an LA County Thomas Guide in cash.

The culture shock of coming back home was worse than it was acclimating to Europe. In Europe, you expected things to be different and strange, but being back "home" was shocking. This was where he was *supposed* to be comfortable, but it wasn't comforting. Here, he was *expected* to fit in, but he didn't. After all, this is the land that created and shaped him, right?

He took the top down and drove along Santa Monica Blvd. to Lincoln. Lunch at Norm's sounded good.

*

Digger ordered a turkey burger combo after he was seated at a table by the Norm's hostess.

He needed a place to live. He looked over the newspaper ads while sitting at the counter.

He spent fistfuls of change making calls from the payphone. By the time an ad came out in the papers, it seemed that the place was already taken. Digger needed a different strategy.

He paid his check and left the restaurant. Digger got into his new car and took out the Thomas Guide. He cruised different local neighborhoods looking for one where he might want to live.

He wound up in an area near Venice called Mar Vista.

After a couple of false starts and dead ends, he saw a "FOR RENT" sign on a white picket fence—no fooling, a *white picket fence*—so he pulled over. He went through the white picket archway's swinging gate to find himself flanked by two rows of bungalows that looked like they were constructed in the 1920s. There were palm trees. This was the stuff of Old Hollywood. One of the front doors on the left was open. Digger entered.

The place was empty. Hmmm. Nicely kept wood floors. Bakelite door handles. Sweet.

The place needed paint, but when Digger saw a dozen cats, sunning themselves on the opposite roof, he was sold.

He called the number that was on the sign from a noisy liquor store payphone on Venice Blvd. He strained to hear over the loud whooshing traffic.

"Yeah?" answered the voice on the other end.

"Hello. I'm calling about 3992 1/2 Inglewood Blvd. I'm quite interested."

"Yeah, sorry, but I got a lot of interest in that property. I'm done showing it—"

"I can bring you six months' rent, plus a first and last, within the half hour."

"Come get the keys."

Chapter 38 - Furniture Shopping

The next morning, Digger woke up on the floor of his brand new empty bungalow apartment, surrounded only by luggage and newspapers. Digger needed furniture.

After a late breakfast at Norm's, he put the top down on the Cabriolet and took PCH south until he hit a stretch of car washes and antique stores. He wanted to make this quick. Well, maybe not *too* quick. He wasn't finicky, but he did have *some* taste.

The first shop was crammed with dusty relics that must have been sitting there for a decade, if a day. It was so packed that slim Digger could not maneuver in between the china cabinets and roll-top desks.

He hopped back into his car and headed a bit farther down PCH, searching for another store.

This is more like it. This was a nice space with extra showrooms in the back. One could stroll through here and test sit a chair for a spell. There were artifacts of Deco, mid-century modern and other antiquity, as well as some more contemporary pieces.

After shopping for an hour, he picked out a desk, desk lamp, a small sofa with rosewood legs and accents, a coffee table, a standing full-length mirror and some copper torchiere floor lamps.

Digger brought his order to the counter, where the merchant began filling out a handwritten receipt.

"Delivery is extra," said the merchant, as if expecting an argument.

"Then you'll make more money, won't you?"

"Will that be cash or—"

"Cash." Digger still had his credit cards and American bank account from before he left the States, but he wasn't certain that he wanted his moves documented just yet.

Next, Digger needed a bed. He remembered a store he'd seen on Pico. He took the 405 freeway north, back up toward his new neck of the woods.

Digger pulled up, parked on the street and fed the meter. Whooshing traffic tousled his hair a bit.

The bell ring-dinged as he pushed through the door. A grid of beds was laid out like white bread sandwiches on a cafeteria tray. He waited for service.

Then, she came in.

He recognized her from the movies. She had red hair and a plump personal assistant who carried a heavy purse, seemingly for the both of them.

Finally, a salesman appeared. "Okay. Who was here first?"

"Ladies first," offered Digger.

"Why aren't you gallant?" offered the personal assistant. She had a slight southern accent.

"We need a bed for our guest room and—oh, I don't know what I want. Why don't you take care of him first?" offered the starlet.

"And you, sir?" the salesman asked Digger.

"I always sleep great in hotels."

"Ah! I have just the thing!" The salesman moved to the center of the store, beckoning Digger to follow him.

"I just sold two hundred of these to the L.A. Sheraton Hotel! Just feel that! Go on. Try it out!"

Digger kicked off his sneakers and scooted onto the bed. He lay on his back, staring at the ceiling.

"You would like the King, yes?"

"No. I don't think so. My new place is pretty small. What else you got?"

"You need a Full," Starlet interjected.

"I do?" responded Digger.

With that, Starlet jumped onto the bed, right alongside Digger. The assistant sat on the edge of the bed next to it.

"Yes. You do! For you and all your female companions!"

"Let's remind ourselves that you are a married woman," said the assistant to deaf ears.

"Oh, I don't know much about that," a modest Digger answered the starlet.

"Sure you do! Look! It's a slumber party!"

"We'd best be going," intervened the assistant. "I got to get your bony ass back for a meeting by four."

Digger went to the salesdesk, paid his bill and scribbled his address.

"Wait! What's your name?" asked the starlet.

"You can call me," Digger leaned in toward her. "Zorro."

Starlet threw her head back and chuckled quietly while her assistant rolled her eyes.

Digger left for his car with a grin.

Chapter 39 - Budget Ballroom

Sitting in his new apartment near dusk, at his new desk, Digger took out the LA Weekly and flipped to the back section until he found a decent-looking club. Digger clubbed just about every night, for weeks at a time when he was in Europe, having acquired a taste for it in Barcelona and Paris. The Weekly had a whole calendar dedicated to such things.

He spotted an ad for ballroom classes in Westwood. Black and white movies of guys in tuxes and gals in evening gowns… He had always wished he could dance like that. To hell with James Bond or Rambo. He wanted to be Gene Kelly.

Digger still knew a little bit. Beverly had taught him a basic box step a few years back at a snooty soiree.

The ad looked elegant, sophisticated, and a tad intimidating. *Better to start with something a little more manageable.*

He opened the Santa Monica Junior College catalog he got in the mail. *Ah, that's better.* Lower the bar a little. He picked up the phone and dialed the number.

*

Digger placed the parking decal on the corner of his windshield. The Summer sky still lit up a fluorescent orange this late into the evening.

He made his way from the parking lot of the community college to the main East Building, clutching his class schedule and enrollment slip. Through the windows, he saw adults,

166

mostly couples, standing about, some practicing basic dance moves. This must be the place. He entered.

Like most everyone else, Digger drifted in a small circle, checking out the fire sprinklers mounted in the ceiling.

It was a large, empty tiled room with a long table near the door.

Suddenly, a man and woman burst into the room. They carried themselves like a pair of figure skaters and had smiles that seemed to have been carved into their faces. The man wearing a scarf placed a boom box on the table.

"Good evening, dancers! I'm Linda!"

"And I'm Tom!"

"And we're going to be your dance sherpas!" they announced in unison.

They banged their hands together rapidly and instructed everybody to form two lines, one for males, one for females. The class then ran through some simple exercises. They rocked from side to side, lifting a foot with each motion, then they shifted their weight from foot to foot, rocking front to back. Digger followed the instructions, although the class seemed to be moving awfully slowly.

Digger had a slight pain in his thigh where the bullet had lodged, but no noticeable effect on his movement.

From what Beverly had shown him, to what he'd picked up, here and there in Europe, Digger knew some of the basics, the box step, some of the turns…

Things picked up, however, when they paired up to do some actual dancing. Some of the couples who came together refused to dance with anybody but the partner they brought. When they were told that was not an option in this class, some left, others reconsidered. Women outnumbered men something like 8-to-1. Digger liked those odds. He, along with the other men, was valued, especially when it was discovered that Digger had a decent sense of rhythm.

The men made a ring around the room, facing inward. The women made a second ring, facing the men. Most of the dancers found it impossible to maintain any semblance of arm tension.

"Come on, dancers! Keep those arms rigid! I don't want to see any drooping Spaghetti Arms!"

Digger sidled up to his first partner of the night. She was a middle-aged woman who smiled politely and nervously as they took up their positions—her hand on his shoulder, his on her shoulder blade.

With the push of a button, the music began. Digger's partner counted out loud and mashed his foot repeatedly. She stared at her feet and hiccuped apologies.

"Okay! Change partners!"

Digger's second partner was also older, but had the allure of a well put-together professional woman. They exchanged names. Hers was Sharon. She wore slacks and a blouse. She seemed comfortable with Digger. They danced the box step without incident for the duration of their time together.

"Hey. Don't go too far away, y'hear?" Sharon said to Digger when they were called to change partners once again.

They took a coffee or smoke break. Sharon and Digger practiced their rhumba. An older couple observed them, asking a question every now and again.

Digger and Sharon showed them that one could dance the rhumba, which was really just the box step, to most popular songs. Sharon and Digger sang song after song in 4/4 time, demonstrating the dance step to the amazement of lookers on.

The other students were in envy over how fast Digger and Sharon seemed to have "gotten it."

They sang to each other songs from Eagles and The Beatles, all while maintaining a steady rhumba.

When break time was over, they all went back inside.

Upon returning to class, they broke back up again into lines of men and women. They were taught a simple underarm turn. Some nodded while others shook their heads. Some did not return from the break.

After the instruction part of class, the teachers turned the students loose in a dance free-for-all. A few of the ladies made a bee-line for Digger, but Sharon had managed to not stray too far from him, so she scooped him up first.

In no time, class was over.

"Give yourselves a big hand!" yelled Linda. "See you Thursday!"

Digger left class and walked to his car.

From the driver's seat he could see Sharon emerge from the building, appearing to look for him. He hit the ignition and drove out of the parking lot.

He wound up dropping the class.

Chapter 40 - Free-Range

At night, this stretch of road had no street lights to expose its secrets. It was the only thing connecting Duarte to Irwindale. It looked like a good place to dump a body or take one's own life. With its sinister expanse, dotted with wild brush, it reminded Digger that California was a desert.

Talk radio was a whole magazine, hosting a variety of shows, ranging from advice for the lovelorn to UFOs, everything for the discriminating insomniac.

Digger drove highly engaged, his hands strangling the steering wheel.

He had gassed up in Monrovia, so he figured that he was pretty much good to go for a while.

He drove the back roads of Sunland, winding, stretching and sprawling roads that led seemingly deeper and deeper into a treacherous nowhere. He was no longer on pavement. He was driving on dirt. No moon, no telephone poles, only headlights.

He passed through a couple of chain link gates, half-expecting shotguns or dogs to materialize. It reminded him of movies that didn't end well.

He checked his gas gauge and used its dropping needle as an excuse to head back toward a freeway. No, it wasn't his mounting fear that tipped the scale. It was the gas.

He drove, hoping he could find his way back.

Chapter 41 - Campus Tour

Like most college campuses, the campus of Fairlight University was seemingly designed to lose, or at least frustrate, its visitors. Digger drove the winding, tree-lined maze toward the visitors' parking lot.

He had made some half-hearted calls to various colleges in Southern California. Why he'd want to stay in the area puzzled even him. He was free and adventurous in Europe, but seemed to be tethered, now that he was back home, to his old ways, his old weaknesses, the way we revert to our younger selves when having Thanksgiving with the folks.

He was being persnickety and he knew it. This was a crisis of identity. Much of his old self was settling back upon him like a full set of infantry gear.

Back on American soil, Digger was hypervigilant, always on the alert. His breathing was shallower. He was more jittery. It was like when he was a kid and it was time for his mother to come home from work. And after all, he was an art forger, con man, and … murderer, back on the soil that knew him best.

Digger locked the door on his Cabriolet, then asked himself, why? Sheer force of habit, it must have been. This place looked lovely and safe, with its big shady oak and jacaranda trees.

He looked over his shoulder, as if being followed, then set off walking the wide pathway toward a large map of the campus. After locating himself on the map, he headed for a cluster of administrative buildings, the whole time taking in the panorama of Academia.

A few twists and turns later, Digger met up with José, Digger's assigned student guide for Fairlight University. José handed Digger a stack of pamphlets, brochures and a thick Fall catalogue.

"So, where did you come from before here?" asked José. José had a head of black wavy hair and the wispy promise of a future moustache. He bobbed from side to side as he and Digger made their way through the campus.

"Mostly Spain," Digger answered.

This *fascinated* José.

"Wow. After travelling all over like that, I think I'd find it hard to come back here."

"My being here baffles me, too."

José showed Digger around the campus, the quad, the library, the classrooms…

When he asked Digger about pledging a fraternity, Digger couldn't suppress a laugh.

"That's okay. I have my own place."

"Really? Want a roommate?" asked José.

"Sorry. I think I'm a little past that."

"Oh. Okay."

They ate at the cafeteria, where José filled Digger in on all of the "hard teachers."

José's words began to echo and recede. Digger drifted quickly and far from this conversation and this location.

When Digger came to, he thanked José and then lied to him, saying that he had a really good time and that he would seriously think about enrolling.

Digger left José and started to make his way back to the parking lot. Gaggles and stragglers of students, criss-crossed the campus. One snagged his eye. She carried a backpack and had large coils of blonde hair. Digger fixed his gaze upon her. When she turned a corner and disappeared through a brick arch, he followed her.

This was one of those times when he wished he could just blend in. But, that was rarely the case. Digger stuck out like an extra thumb. It wasn't just his clothing. Something about him just magnetized people's eyes. He always thought he'd make a lousy spy.

Despite all that, he just could not seem to help himself.

He followed her, swinging his Fairlight catalog as if it were a textbook.

She headed toward the bookstore. She entered. He followed.

Once inside, Digger momentarily dropped his tailing her. He looked around, browsed and perused. He checked out the books, the sweatshirts and the coffee mugs. While he was looking at a carousel of Cliff's Notes, he saw her again. She was now in the checkout line.

He got in line behind her. Without a purchase item, he was nervous. He needed a reason to be in this line.

When she approached the cashier, Digger reached past her and grabbed a pen that had a school emblem on it, from the display can.

Her hair smelled good.

They exchanged rather neutral looks, then she completed her purchase and walked away and out of the automatic doors.

Digger put the pen back and told the cashier, "Changed my mind."

He exited the bookstore and looked around. He saw her about fifty yards away.

He shook off his thoughts of this young woman. He had to.

Digger power walked to his car. He dumped the Fairlight catalog in a trash can along the way. He realized that he would be claustrophobic in any American university. He wanted something and was not afraid to work for it. Digger just could not imagine where to begin to find it.

The clock was ticking. A weight was pressing upon him. Digger could not name it.

Chapter 42 - Hitting the Stacks

Digger entered the Venice library. If he couldn't bring himself to formal education, he was going to have to go about educating himself.

The patrons were not the only thing occupying it. The hush took up the airspace. It was a real, tangible thing. You could touch it.

He thought of his former friend Kevin. Kevin read everything within his grasp. Everything.

Digger aimlessly mined the stacks until he stumbled upon the Classics section. And why not? It was too often that during conversations he was caught feeling lost, not knowing widely exchanged references. He hated that feeling.

He grabbed books by Shakespeare, Mark Twain and Upton Sinclair, as well as those on Greek and Roman Mythology, American and World History from the shelves.

Once again, Digger had no real idea what he was doing.

He thought of looking up Kevin. However, Kevin was now in the Army, stationed who knows where.

He sidled up to the counter and waited to be waited on. A woman with a macramé vest and hair that evaded the word "style" approached him. A jar with a slitted lid and some coins and a few bills in it sat on the counter. A piece of paper that read "Friends of the Library" was inexpertly taped to it.

"Yes, hello! I'd like a library card!" said Digger with extra pep.

The woman lit up like a lit up woman.

176

"That's wonderful! I'll just need some ID and a utility bill and 25 cents."

"I don't really have a utility bill. I just moved in."

The cheerful librarian looked perplexed, as if having to choose a medical procedure.

"Oh, heck. I can vouch for you. I mean, you're not some kind of Boston Strangler, are you?"

"No, ma'am. Never been to Boston." Digger folded up ten dollars and stuffed it into the jar.

"Oh! Well, that's a relief!" She stamped all of the books.

"There you go. Due back in two weeks. You're all set."

He left the library and drove across town to Kevin's house.

Digger rang the doorbell. It sounded harsh and raspy, like it had a short in it. There was a large ceramic frog next to the door. The door opened.

"Digger! I can't believe it's you! I was so surprised to get your call! Come in!"

Kevin's mom was an itty bitty thing with dyed black hair and thick eyeglasses. She wore *huarache* sandals and pedal pusher pants.

She offered Digger something to drink and proceeded to interrogate him on what he'd been doing for the past few years.

"Oh, you know. This and that. I went on a study trip to Spain," Digger half-truthed.

"You know, I think that Kevin mentioned something about that program. I wanted him to go, but, well… you know Kevin."

Kevin's mom took a sip of her wine cooler. Digger refilled his cup of water from the *jarra* on the table.

"Kevin, as you probably know, is wrapping up his enlistment."

"Yeah, I was thinking of going out to Kentucky to see him. Do you think that's a bad idea?"

"Bad idea? Heck, no! You two have been best friends since… well, since forever!"

Digger got the phone number and mailing address for Kevin in Kentucky, then thanked Kevin's mom with a hug. She invited him to come back anytime.

Digger left the house and got into his car.

Digger had declined Kevin's mom's offer for food, but now he was getting peckish and jittery. He didn't much feel like the empty camaraderie of a sit-down restaurant, so he just picked up a sandwich and fries at the Carl's Jr. "drive-thru," then gassed up.

He drove the freeways, listening to the local NPR nighttime music line-up, eating his modest fast food meal. The food in Paris and in Catalonia was not to be believed. But, you know, this was good, too. It was simple. Roast beef with pepper jack cheese and an ortega chile. Not too bad.

Digger loved the freeways at night. There was something meditative about driving them.

After cruising for hours, he drove uphill by Beverly's house but did not stop. The lights were on and there were two cars in the driveway.

He took a small stack of library books to Norm's on Lincoln. They were open 24 hours and had that turkey burger combo.

Digger studied all night until sunrise. He was adrift and it was getting old. He wanted to establish something, to put down some roots. He wanted to touch something. He wanted something to touch him.

Chapter 43 - Kentucky

Digger had no idea how long his stay might be, so he bought a round-trip ticket to Kentucky with an open return time. He got himself a motel room near the base, Fort Knox. He joked to himself, *They're letting Kevin stay near all that gold?*

He waited until the next day to call the base. Kevin's mom had said that he happened to be between bivouacs— military campouts— so chances to catch him were good.

Well, not that good. Digger left a message.

He read some, then steeped himself in the motel pool like a tea bag. The room had free HBO. Well, what do ya' know?

When Digger and Kevin finally connected, it was only to make arrangements to meet. There was no warmth, no, "Hey, how are ya?"

That was sort of understandable under the circumstances. They had been childhood best friends who just seemed to drift apart, became less and less of a priority to each other.

They met at the Flying J diner, just off base, a place Digger assumed Kevin frequented. They had a long counter and ceiling fans. Digger, arriving first, secured them a booth.

Kevin was there at noon, right on the dot. He slid into the booth wearing his BDUs (Battle Dress Uniform). He ordered a huge meal: pancakes, chicken fried steak and eggs, hash browns and coffee.

A good sign, Digger thought. Breaking bread, like old times. This wouldn't be just a quick "Fuck you."

Digger asked about Kevin's MOS, Military Occupational Specialty.

"Why? Why now, Digger?" Kevin's voice had the tiniest inflection of a Kentuckian dialect. Digger had noticed a change in his own inflection, now back in the States. Funny how being in a different environment brings out the contrasts.

"Why now? Because that's what time it is. The time is now."

"What a Digger answer." Kevin sat up straighter than Digger had ever seen. He now had military posture.

Digger reached for the salt and knocked over his ice water. He felt a flash of rage, embarrassment and self-loathing. He scooped up the ice and wiped up the water with some paper napkins, lightning-fast. Digger thought about his mother. He always thought about his mother. He did this just about every waking moment. *How would she want me to do this? Would she disapprove of that?* She was the context as well as the metric of all of his behavior.

"Man, it's real simple. I miss you. Do you still want to be my friend or not?"

"Not." Kevin spoke in that clipped, military way.

"Have we changed that much, Kevin?"

"I don't know about me, but you have."

Digger thought for a minute.

"You're probably right. But can't you be friends with the guy in front of you?"

"I don't want to," confirmed Kevin.

"Well, I guess there's nothing I can do."

"And another thing, Digger."

"Yeah?"

"Leave my mother alone."

Chapter 44 - Reconnecting

Walking along the nearly deserted Venice boardwalk in the morning was for locals. It was too early for tourists. There was a lot of dog walking. A few actors. Digger brought a Walkman radio to listen to the KIIS FM morning show with Rick Dees.

He thought about Kevin's rejection to resuming their friendship. Kevin either was still hurt or had simply learned to live without his camaraderie. Digger regretted his part of their falling out.

They had grown up together, used to have late night pow-wows at Carrows to study and cram while in junior college. Then, Digger drifted away from the JC, spending more and more time at Design Center. Kevin, having no money for college, just like Digger, made the painful decision to join the Army for the GI Bill, despite his long-standing history as a pacifist. These things caused a rift that eventually became an unmendable ripping apart.

Digger practiced his ballroom steps on the cement. He thought of Beverly. He thought of the Valentine's gift he gave her, three years ago.

Dini Topp. Beverly hated Dini Topp. *Digger* hated Dini Topp. Dini Topp was Beverly's—and Digger's—mortal enemy. She had been an admissions administrator at Design Center.

Digger had grown close to Beverly while a night student at the school. She was a lonely woman who, she thought, had lost her husband and toddler daughter. On a camping trip, she had been in the position of having to choose—save the husband or save the child. She chose and her husband did not forgive her.

Dini Topp was rude. She was cruel. She had represented everything that Digger and Beverly found wrong with the world and she was influencing class after class of students whom she would have believe that "Kent State" was only a song by Crosby, Stills, Nash & Young.

Digger would stand for her no longer. He killed her so that his friend Beverly could take her influential job at Design Center. Of course, Beverly never knew of any of this until after the fact. She was likely the only person on Earth to know who killed Dini Topp, although she actually had no real proof. After her murder, Digger had boarded that plane bound for Spain.

He snapped out of these thoughts as he approached Norm's. The place had become his regular go-to for convenient eats. He thought of it like a school cafeteria.

The wait staff of all shifts recognized him. An iced tea was waiting for him as he took his seat at the counter.

After polishing off his chicken-fried steak and eggs, Digger got on the 10 FWY and pointed his convertible toward Pasadena.

Digger pulled his car up to Design Center. He parked in one of the four visitors' spaces.

He passed by a flock of art students who looked too young to be there, then headed toward Administration. He bypassed reception and went to Dini Topp's old office.

There she was, his old friend. Beverly wore a tailored business suit. She was looking over some papers spread across her desk when she looked up and saw him in the doorway.

"Good god."

Beverly rounded the table and hugged him. She hugged him tightly.

"Oh, Digger! I've missed you, thought a lot about you since you left."

It was great to see her but it wasn't the same. Something was off. *You can't go home again.*

There was a certain romance to friendships. Sometimes, a friendship couldn't survive the introduction (or re-introduction) of an intimate addition, a boyfriend, girlfriend, a spouse.

Once Peter returned, Beverly's life just couldn't accommodate Digger anymore. That tender, vulnerable, intimate piece of her went back to her husband.

They regarded each other for a long and awkward silence until Beverly asked Digger, "Have you eaten?"

They bought lunch in the cafeteria, but took it outside. Digger let his food just sit there, since he'd had a large and late breakfast.

"I'll never forget what you did for me, Digger."

"I wish you would."

"Right."

Digger filled Beverly in on his recent adventures.

"You should come back here. Full-time, Digger. You're too good."

"I'm too old," he joked.

"I'm serious."

"I'm not certain this is the place for me. Too many ghosts. Too many memories. Too many loose ends."

Beverly said she understood. From there, the silence was uncomfortable. The discomfort grew too sad, so Digger and Beverly said their goodbyes and went their separate ways.

Chapter 45 - Cruise Control

Digger's car ran the streets of Santa Monica like the ball in one of those small handheld games in which the little bead rolls around until the player tilts it into its target divot. He prowled aimlessly, piloting his Cabriolet whose cab glowed red by the stereo light, giving Digger the feeling that he was in a darkroom or a submarine.

He slowed down as he passed the Laemmle movie theatre. It was showing *Cinema Paradiso, The Unbearable Lightness of Being* and *Women on the Verge of a Nervous Breakdown*. However, the theater was dark as it was well after midnight.

Digger came to a stop. One of the display cases was slightly open. Whoever last changed the posters must not have locked it. The one-sheet in question was for *Cinema Paradiso*.

He left the car running and hopped out, trotting to the glassy display case. Digger looked both ways. The coast was mainly clear. He opened the case and removed the huge poster.

He hurriedly rolled it up as he returned to his car. He tossed the poster into the back seat and drove off.

Add thief to the list, he thought to himself. He felt an electric current flow through him; half guilt, half thrill.

Cruising back up Lincoln, Digger saw a woman in a heavy jacket walking along the sidewalk. Upon seeing his headlights, she turned and stuck her thumb out. He pulled over.

His thoughts raced and his fantasies flew. He could kill this woman. There would be no way to connect them, he thought. He panicked. Were his darkest impulses finally merging with his actions?

From his figure drawing classes, he had seen just about every body type nude. Digger could easily picture what violating and devouring this woman would look like. He could hear the crunch of her soft tissue as it burst between his clenching teeth. Hear her breathing.

"I live just down the street and my feet are killing me. Could I get a ride?" the woman asked.

"Sure. Hop in," said Digger.

She stared straight ahead as she spoke. "I'm Stacy."

"Me too," Digger joked. She laughed.

"I'm Digger."

"Pleased to meet you, Digger." Stacy now looked at Digger as she spoke. She wiggled out of her jacket. She must have been in her late thirties.

Digger forced his eyes on the road as they wanted to run amok over his passenger's body.

They chatted. Light stuff.

"Oh here. This is me," Stacy said.

Digger pulled to the curb in front of a charming two-story.

"Thanks for the ride, Digger."

"Sure. Anytime."

Stacy sat there for longer than Digger expected.

"You wouldn't want to come in, would you?"

"Sure. I'd like that," Digger said, smiling, not believing his luck. He was panting inside.

They climbed the front stairs and entered her house. A large Rottweiler approached them, barking at a moderate volume. Digger was scared. Stacy grabbed the dog in a bear hug around the neck.

"Let me just put him in the bathroom," she said. "Have a seat on the sofa. I'll be right back."

When Stacy reemerged, she was braless, wearing a T-shirt and sweatpants. She threw a sheer scarf over a lamp, turning the whole living room a burnt peach color. She put some music on way down low.

The two sat on the sofa. She offered him wine.

"Just a little. Gotta drive," said Digger.

"Right."

Digger gave her a foot rub.

They moved to the bedroom where Stacy removed her shirt for a back rub. She laid on her belly while Digger kneaded and squeezed her. Her breasts bulged out the sides and he caressed them.

She returned the favor, squeezing groans out of his trapezius muscles.

Stacy's bed had a sturdy, wrought iron headboard one could really get a hold of. She bucked and strained as Digger reamed her in the blue non-light. With each noise she made, the dog in the bathroom right next to them scraped, scratched and growled at the door all the more.

"Down, Zeus! Shut up!" Stacy hissed.

Digger wanted to bite her nipples off. The dog barked. Digger wanted to ball up his fist and strike her, strike her in the face. He wanted to crush that face. The dog barked louder. Digger was terrified.

Stacy went down on him and let him finish in her mouth, then they both nodded off.

Digger woke up having to use the bathroom, but remembered that Zeus the Rottweiler was caged in there. He whispered goodbye to a half-asleep Stacy who groaned something like "Bye, Digger."

Digger locked the door behind him as he left Stacy's house. He reached his car to find a thirty-five-dollar parking ticket at 5:30 am.

He headed to Norm's for some breakfast.

Chapter 46 - Olivia

Digger went to the 7:30 ballroom class in Westwood. It was only 6:45. He sat in his car, waiting for the teachers to arrive. Digger wanted to attend a decent college or university but hated rich kids. That ruled out schools like USC and Design Center. He seemed to get along just fine with the wealthy in Europe. There was just something he hated about rich Americans. It wasn't jealousy. It was something else. Boorishness. Yes, that was it.

He didn't know what he wanted in the Big Picture, but he also didn't want to waste away while figuring it out. Furthering his formal education seemed like the best thing to do in the meantime, but that was proving problematic.

The ballroom teachers finally opened the doors and let in the line of people waiting.

Digger handed over his $35 and took his sports jacket to the coat check. The circular ballroom was spectacular with its various wooden inlays and stained glass ceiling. It was the stuff of movie musicals. It was glorious. Nothing like the clunky lessons at the community college.

According to the ad in the LA Weekly, the first part of the evening was a basic lesson, then an open dance party.

Digger concentrated on following directions. He kept his "carriage" rigid. He looked over his partner's right shoulder and led his partner confidently.

The male part of the teacher team clapped his hands together to get the attention of the room.

"Remember, gentlemen, you only have one job, and that is to keep your partner from bumping into anyone or anything."

The teacher gave the direction to change partners. Digger was next paired with a sour older woman who regarded Digger as if he smelled. She had the relaxed comfort of a regular. She would not look at him when he introduced himself. Perhaps, she disapproved of his attire. Digger wore a T-shirt and trousers.

"You're all sweaty!" she exclaimed, rather exaggeratedly. Her pinched face was one that looked like it had sent back many a soup.

"I'm sorry. I apologize," said Digger.

When it was time to rotate partners, she scoffed and left in a huff.

Digger now stood in front of a young woman who made him gasp.

She captivated Digger. She didn't have one of those supermodel faces that oh, so bored him. Her features were arranged in a way that simply fascinated him. Her green-hazel eyes had a cool intelligence to them. They resembled the eyes from peacock feathers. Her oiled hair was pulled straight back into a tidy bun as she presented herself to Digger. Digger introduced himself by offering his hand.

"Hi. Digger."

"Olivia." She said, accepting the handshake.

"I'm afraid I'm only a beginner. Sorry for the sweat."

"Sorry? For sweat? It's a *dance class*."

"Exactly! Still, I feel kinda underdressed," confessed Digger.

"Underdressed? Wearing a Louis Vuitton no logo T-shirt and tailored slacks? Those shoes are fine Italian leather."

"You noticed."

"I did. You're the best-dressed man here."

The music started and they launched into their waltz.

"I don't know if I can stay too long. I'm under a work crunch. You wouldn't happen to know anybody who does storyboards, would you?" Olivia joked.

They danced. It felt like real dancing, not classroom fumbling, not homework.

"Storyboards?" Digger asked flatly, without losing his rhythm.

"Storyboards. They're drawings," she explained. "They're used in TV and movies to figure out how particular scenes are to be shot." The music stopped and time for a break was called.

"Here, follow me." The participants slowly scattered and headed for either the rest rooms or the refreshment tables.

Digger and Olivia went out to her car, a spiffy Mercedes. She pulled a large sheaf of long pages out from the passenger side. They had Post-It Notes sticking out from them.

He scanned the pages like a machine. Each sheet had three frames across with captions beneath them. He'd heard of storyboards before, but had never really known much about them.

"I could do this," Digger concluded.

"You could?" said Olivia in disbelief. "You draw?"

"Sure. It's just like comics, right? Straight storytelling." Digger pointed to the various panels. "You got your establishing shot, your close-up, your product shot... Sure."

192

"I guess you're right, Digger. Hey, come with me after class."

"You got it."

Over coffee and a late-night meal, Olivia gave Digger a brief crash course in storyboarding.

"See these arrows in the corners of the frame pointing outward?" asked Olivia.

"Yeah."

"Those mean that the camera pulls back. If the arrows are pointing inward, toward the center of the frame, that means that the camera pushes or 'zooms' in."

"What do I need to bring in the way of supplies?" asked Digger, nodding.

"Don't worry. We've got all that stuff at work. Markers, tracing paper. The works."

Olivia gave Digger her card. "Show up at ten?"

"You bet."

"It should be fun. And, the money's good."

Chapter 47 - Intro to Storyboards

The next day, Digger appeared at Hawkins and Marsh, Olivia's work, where she greeted him at the reception desk and showed him around.

She looked as good as she did at the previous night's ballroom class. She was probably the most fashionable American woman he'd ever been in the same room with. She still wore her hair in that stylish and sexy bun. Digger's heart went giddy-up, but he tried not to let on.

"There's the copy machine. Now, the way I've seen it done is, the illustrators make the line drawings on tracing paper, then marker the copies." They were like co-conspirators, trying to get away with something. It was fun.

"Makes sense," Digger replied.

"All of our offices are full. I'll set you up in the conference room. Oh, make sure to get your parking validated. Ali, the director should be with you shortly. I'll pop in and out, make sure you're okay. Alright?"

"Sure beats clubbing in Spain," Digger joked. Olivia made a face like he had flicked water at her, as if she wasn't sure she'd heard him right.

Digger picked up the script that lay on the table and flipped through it.

A hard-jawed young man poked his head into the room. Behind him stood Olivia.

"This him?"

"Yes, Clifford. This is Digger. Digger, this is Clifford."

"The director," Digger assumed.

"No, no. Not me. Thanks for coming in on such short notice." said Clifford, addressing Digger as if he were here to wash his car. He wore a tie.

Clifford was conventionally handsome with a dimpled chin. Digger thought his eyes were just a tad too close together.

"Sure. My pleasure," answered Digger.

With that, Clifford disappeared. Digger was glad. Clifford put off a definite vibe and not a good one.

Olivia had a production assistant bring in a *huge* tower of Prismacolor markers. There must have been a couple of hundred of them. The PA took Digger to the supply closet where he loaded up on various pencils, tracing paper, marker paper, a plastic triangle and an electric pencil sharpener.

Again, Digger looked over the script. He was lost, in over his head. He felt like a fraud. This was all going to blow any minute. He felt naked.

Ali, the director, entered, breaking Digger's concentration. He was a small, wiry man with a grand view of himself.

"Okay, what we have here is your basic cough syrup spot. Only this time—"

Digger took notes as the director spoke. He took them mainly in the form of tiny thumbnail sketches drawn on the margins of the script. He would show them to the fast-talking director periodically.

"Dynamite," "Perfect," "Exactly," the director would answer.

"Here, we rotate the camera counterclockwise—" instructed the director.

"So, that the image goes clockwise," said Digger, completing the thought.

"No. Counterclockwise."

"But, if you turn the camera counterclockwise, the image goes clockwise," corrected Digger.

"Don't argue with me! I've been directing for *four years*!"

Digger suppressed a chuckle. Four years? Four years seemed pretty puny when he thought of the age and experience of his mentors, guys like Walt and Pashone. Digger had drawn with guys who worked on *Fantasia*.

When they were both confident that Digger had his marching orders, the director got up from his chair.

"This has to be right, you understand," said Ali in a panic. "We are way over budget and behind schedule."

"You can go put out other fires. This is taken care of," Digger assured the director.

These words actually seemed to put the director at ease.

Digger was grateful to work unsupervised. His first attempts were… disastrous, really. Just for a moment, he panicked. *Luckily, I work fast,* he thought. He had time to make mistakes or to find his sea legs.

Olivia stuck her head in.

"How's everything going? You hungry? We're sending out for lunch. Gyros."

"Everything's great," Digger replied, scrambling to cover his work, but happy to see Olivia.

"Good. By the way, Ali loves you."

Digger was astonished to hear these words. "He does? Well, I hope he does after he sees the work."

"I'm sure he will." Olivia dismissed herself.

Digger got back to the business of figuring out this storyboard mess. He just told himself to breathe. *Just like comics. This is just like comics. Just tell the story.*

He roughed out the whole story according to the script and drew it on regular copy paper. Digger would make the drawings pretty later, probably using tracing paper. That was when the wiry director popped in.

"Hey! How's it going?"

"Uh, great! Not quite ready for inspection yet—"

"Let's take a look."

Ali laid out all of the rough pages in sequence on the table. His hand hovered above them as he "read" the 'boards."

Digger was terrified. He resigned himself to failure, rehearsing his apology in his head.

"Love it," he concluded. "Clean 'em up and get 'em to the PA and you're done."

He shook Digger's hand. "Thanks, rock star. You really saved the day." The director then left the room.

Digger saluted the empty room, then set out to follow the director's orders.

He slipped a rough drawing beneath the top sheet of tracing paper, then used a black Prismacolor pencil and Sharpie marker to draw a tighter, more refined version of a sick little girl, lying in bed.

After he'd "cleaned up" each drawing, Digger shot Xeroxes of them. He took the Xeroxes back to the desk. He grabbed a marker from the large set brought to him earlier. He added tone to the little girl's hair and face.

Oh shit.

The marker had bled through the copy paper, ruining the copy underneath. *Won't be doing that again,* Digger thought to himself. He shot new copies and turned the tracing paper pad cardboard side up, using it as a blotter.

Digger finished all of the boards and spent a few minutes just admiring them before calling the PA over to accept them.

He did it. He pulled it off.

Olivia entered the room.

"Here. I figured you didn't have your own invoices so I wrote these up." Olivia handed Digger some papers, then spoke to him in a hushed, conspiratorial tone. "You know, you did amazingly well for someone who'd never drawn a storyboard in his life."

"Like I said, it was just like comics."

Clifford entered the room.

"Hey doll. I got to take care of something, so I'll just meet you at the restaurant."

She nodded. He went to kiss her, but just got her cheek.

Oh, great, thought Digger. *They're a couple. Just great.*

Chapter 48 - Final Dining

Clifford and Olivia were at an upscale restaurant. Lots of mirrors, dark wood and leather seats.

"Separate checks," Clifford told the waiter. "Just kidding." The waiter didn't laugh. His mouth tightened into a straight line at the remark.

"This is the kind of charm that made me fall for you in the first place," said Olivia sarcastically.

"And, can we get a couple of drinks first?"

"Clifford, I'm out." Olivia interrupted Clifford's banter with the waiter.

"What are you talking about, Olivia?" Clifford panicked. He knew exactly what she was talking about.

"I'm not going. I'm staying put at Hawkins and Marsh."

"Olivia, you can't back out now."

"Now is precisely the time to back out. Now, before things go too far."

The waiter told them he'd be back when they were ready to order.

"You know that we can't do this without—"

"My money?"

"I wasn't gonna say that."

"But, you're thinking that."

Clifford leaned back in his chair. A smile spread across his face. "Maybe, among other things." This is what he liked about Olivia. No bullshit.

"It's not just me we're talking about here. What about the other guys? The guys who we're taking along with us? Those guys are loyal guys," Olivia said, taking a drink of her water.

"They all still have jobs at Hawkins and Marsh. Nobody has been stupid enough to announce anything about us starting our own agency, yet."

"Maybe, almost nobody."

"No, Clifford. You didn't."

"Of course, I didn't, you ninny!" joked Clifford, quite pleased with himself. "By the way, I think we should stop seeing each other."

"Oh, Clifford. Stop it." Clifford knew how much Olivia hated his "sense of humor."

"I'm serious." Clifford did not smirk anymore. "I need a partner I can rely upon."

"Okay. But listen to me, Clifford. You're not taking it back this time."

Clifford just grinned. "Waiter? I'll have the Clams Casino."

Chapter 49 - One of the Crew

A few days later, Olivia called Digger in to Hawkins and Marsh for more work.

"I thought I was getting you out of a one-time jam. I didn't realize I was signing onto the crew," Digger joked as he set up shop in the office Olivia had procured for him.

"What can I say? They like you." Olivia said, then added, "Well, truth is, nobody wants to work with us, not with my team anyway. They're all put off by the director and especially by Clifford."

"Are things really that bad?"

"They are. They are really that bad. They seem to like you, though, which is a good thing, at least for me."

Digger found the work engaging and he wanted to be around Olivia. Hell, it was something to do, something to fill his time other than wandering and obsessing.

She smiled at Digger with what could have been affection before disappearing. Digger reminded himself—this was L.A., where sincerity was the one thing that anyone could fake.

Chapter 50 - See You There

Digger saw Olivia again at ballroom class. He had been once since they had met. Classes ran on Tuesdays and Thursdays, but Olivia only went on Thursdays.

Digger tried not to look as if he were a puppy out to paw at her knees. He wanted to play it cool at work and he saw no reason to stop now.

He stood by the refreshment table until class was set to begin, but, to his surprise and delight, Olivia made a straight shot for him.

"Hey, you," Olivia greeted Digger.

"Hey, you."

"Want to practice a bit until class starts?"

"You bet."

With that, Digger assumed a dance posture and Olivia slipped into place, clasping his left hand.

There was no music so Digger counted off. "1, 2, 3, 2, 2, 3..." and they launched into a simple waltz, smoothly. They glided. They moved together, as one unit, their heads rising and falling, rising and falling. They rotated slightly as they made their way across the floor. A couple of times, Digger kept them from colliding with idle chatters. Bystanders began to take note, including the sour little lady who had scoffed at Digger the previous week.

When the teacher announced the beginning of class over the PA system, Digger and Olivia received a small round of applause from those near them. They broke their position with one another and turned their attention to the instructors.

"Why isn't Clifford here?" Digger whispered to Olivia.

She scoffed. "Clifford? Here? You don't know Clifford. I couldn't *drag* him here."

Digger delighted in that answer. They hushed when the instructors made it a point to say that there was to be no chatting during instruction.

They joined the grand circle and practiced the waltz with every other-gendered person in the place until it was time for the dance party portion of the evening.

Lights dimmed and the room thickened with folks just arriving, folks who didn't need lessons, folks dressed for the evening.

Over the PA, the instructors encouraged the students to dance with as many different partners as possible. "It really makes a big difference in your learning."

A lovely woman in a shimmering dress and sweeping hair asked Digger if he'd care to dance.

"I'm really not very good, I'm afraid."

"Oh, let's see about that."

The speakers piped out *Fly Me to the Moon*, a foxtrot, and Digger's nerves got the better of him. He found himself counting aloud, losing the beat, dropping his arms…

Without a word, the woman excused herself from Digger before the song even ended.

Olivia snuck up on him.

"Hey sailor, dime a dance?"

He chuckled and took up a proper dance frame, his head held high, his back straight. He found his lost confidence. Olivia gave him that.

They spent most of the evening dancing together. Now and then, they would dance with others. Digger's nerves were gone. As long as he stuck to basic moves, with a simple turn here and there, he was smooth and in command, never letting his partner near disaster. Digger became popular quickly as ballroom events usually had men in short supply.

When the night was over, Digger walked Olivia to her car. They rushed ahead of the mostly older crowd who moved like an army of ants toward their cars.

They reached her Mercedes.

"See you next week?" asked Digger.

"If not sooner!"

Chapter 51 - Laurie

Digger got up early and hit the laundromat.

While his clothes were being washed, he got some Mexican breakfast next door then went for a jog while they were in the dryer.

Back home, Digger got a strange call.

"Yeah, hi. This is Meg Frewer. I'm calling from Project X Productions. Do you do storyboards?"

"I guess I do."

"Oh good. I got this number from Georgina, a PA at Hawkins and Marsh. She said you were good. I have a job that starts tomorrow. Are you available?"

Digger went to an art supply store in Santa Monica and loaded up on grayscale markers, tracing paper and some other things. He bought an aluminum attaché case and a clipboard to prop it up from the inside, so that it served as a tabletop easel, so that the flat angle of the conference room table wouldn't distort the drawings. He thought that if he added a lip by gluing a length of L-bracket to it, that would give him a ledge to keep paper from sliding off.

He brought his purchases to the register.

"There he is. The last customer of my shift." The cashier with a blue apron studied Digger's face. "Wait. Didn't you go to Design Center?" She was about Digger's age, with long brown hair and big, round glasses. He didn't recognize her. Digger didn't like not recognizing people.

"No. I might have taken a night class."

"Thought I recognized you. Are you a student, teacher or professional? That way you get a discount. Hell, I'll give you my employee discount. It's better that way anyway." She rang him up.

"Wow."

"Wow, what?" she asked.

"Your cheeks. They're perfect. Perfect coloring. Perfect shape. You're like… a painting."

She went watermelon red.

The cashier bagged his merchandise and handed it to him.

"Got a girlfriend?" she asked.

*

The cashier's name was Laurie. Her bed was a white four-poster. She moaned a lot.

Digger realized that he liked afternoon sex. It had a mellow quality to it. He felt lazy afterward.

Olivia was not an option, so he had broken no loyalty, although he really would have preferred to save himself for an available Olivia. He felt a twinge of guilt.

"You got plans, Digger?" Laurie asked, scooping herself into her brassiere.

"Like what am I gonna do with my life?"

"Oh no," Laurie laughed. "Even I couldn't pass that inspection. I meant what are you doing tonight?" Laurie stepped into a pair of white bib coveralls, like painters wear.

"No plans."

"Wanna go dancing?"

Laurie drove an old Ford Pinto. Loved computers. Programmed primarily in Basic, C++ and S-Plus. Had a TRS 80, a Vic Commodore 64 and a Tandy 1000-TL. She liked

Monty Python. Nice girl. She mostly gave up painting after graduating Design Center.

Dancing should be fun.

They headed up Santa Monica Blvd. toward Hollywood.

"You'd like my friend Kevin," predicted Digger. "Just don't let him anywhere near your computers. He'll take 'em apart and try to put 'em back together."

"He sounds like a blast! When can I meet him?"

"Oh, we're not speaking right now."

"Why's that?" She turned onto Hollywood Blvd. then down a small side street.

"He says that I've changed."

"Well, I like what you've changed into." Laurie gave Digger a playful shove.

She parked at an after-hours meter and turned the car off.

They got out and walked.

"The parking lot at the club is expensive, the valets go through your stuff and you can't get your car out when the club is really going," Laurie explained. "This is better."

They passed a huge mural of a movie audience. Everyone in the audience was a movie star. There was Charlie Chaplin, Marilyn Monroe, Shirley Temple, Humphrey Bogart and Laurel and Hardy, just to name a few. There were over a hundred of them.

As they approached their destination, Laurie grabbed Digger's hand and pulled him along into a run.

"You're gonna love this place! They only play '60s, '70s, Old Soul, Funk and Disco!"

Digger just smiled. It really did sound like fun!

They turned onto Cahuenga Blvd. and there it was, The Crush Bar. The outside was painted all black and purple like a big block of bruise.

Laurie knew the girl who collected admission by name and the big guy who worked the door.

"No, I insist," said Digger as he pulled a few bills from his wallet and laid them before the door girl.

"But I asked *you* out!" Laurie chuckled, "That's not fair!" Laurie scanned the half-filled main room. "What time is it?"

Now that they were inside the darkened club, Digger strained to make the time out on the Swatch he bought in Italy.

"10:05." answered Digger.

"Still a bit early yet. Crowd should get here anytime now. Come on!"

Laurie led Digger to the sparsely filled dance floor just as Cheryl Lynn's *Got to Be Real* started. Laurie's shoulders and hips dipped and swung. Digger then followed, moving from side to side like a Latin lover from the movies. Each performed rather admirably. They could see themselves in the wall of mirrors. They looked good together. They had rhythm and, most importantly, they had enthusiasm. The song went through them and lifted them, carried them.

Digger surprised Laurie. Most guys had to be dragged onto a dance floor when it was packed, let alone when it was so sparse. He wasn't self-conscious. At least, not in this way. Laurie raised her hands above her head and danced. She danced and danced. For two songs, she hopped up on one of the stages and shook it like a go-go dancer. She beckoned for Digger to join her, but he declined.

They were playful on the dance floor, making faces, spinning around and mouthing the lyrics to many of the songs.

They tipped the DJ and he played their favorites. He played Gloria Gaynor's version of *Never Can Say Goodbye* and Stevie Wonder's *Do I Do*.

By now, the crowd was getting thick and the music dwarfed all other sound. Digger made the pantomime gesture of drinking and Laurie nodded. She stayed at the DJ booth and waited for him as he headed across the undulating pool of dancers for the bar.

Wedging his way through the crowd, Digger noticed a couple of movie actors. One was from The Karate Kid II. He looked as plenty scary in person as he did in the movie.

When he reached the bar, Digger shouted, "Excuse me?" to the bartenders to no avail. He was bumped, pushed and shoved by the mob of bar patrons, all thirsty for a drink.

Digger took out a ten-dollar bill and folded it lengthwise. He waved it to get the attention of the nearest bartender, a skinny, stringy blonde with blue glitter on her eyelids and a braless black tank top bearing the club's logo across the chest. She looked directly at Digger, handed out a few bottled beers then leaned in to face him. "Okay! What'll y'have?"

Digger had neglected to find out what Laurie wanted.

"A Corona and a Diet Coke!" he shouted.

"That'll be six bucks!"

Digger slapped the ten down on the bar. "Keep it!"

The bartender slid his drinks to him like casino chips and he walked the drinks back, nearly spilling the soda when someone crashed into him.

When he returned to the DJ booth, where he'd left Laurie, she was nowhere to be found.

From where he stood, he scanned the dance floor, with its mirrored balls, fog machine and throbbing lights.

Digger put the drinks on the booth railing that said, "NO DRINKS," so his hands wouldn't warm them. He just stood there and grooved to a couple of songs when he saw Laurie in the distance, waving her hand straight above her head. She neared Digger and he picked up the drinks from the railing.

"Corona," Digger yelled, leaning into her ear, "and Diet Coke." He presented both to her.

"Is there rum in that?" asked Laurie.

"No!'

Laurie opted for the bottle of Corona. Digger took half of the soda down in one gulp.

"Thanks, Digger! I was in the ladies room." She shouted directly in his ear.

Later on, on the dance floor, they began to lose steam and simultaneously voted to call it quits.

They headed out of the club into the warm summer night and strolled the Walk of Fame. Together, they wondered about the stars from old time radio, whom they did not recognize. They passed a wino, sitting on the sidewalk of Hollywood Blvd, just outside Silvio's Pizza.

Digger and Laurie went in and got two pepperoni slices to go. While Digger was about to pay, he ordered a third slice which he offered to the wino outside.

They walked down the block and around the corner to where she'd parked.

It was all so nice.

"Thanks for this, Laurie! I. Had. A. Blast."

"Digger?

"Yes?"

"Would you kiss me?"

He did. It was nice.

Chapter 52 - Project X

Digger sat on the sofa in the waiting area as instructed while a reel of Project X Productions' work ran on a loop on the monitors. It was in a beautiful old building with exposed brick and pipes.

This production studio specialized in movie trailers. Their client list was as blockbuster as it was exclusive. They did all of the big movies, as well as the movies that made a "statement."

He was twenty-five minutes early. This was his first gig without Olivia as his training wheels and guard rails. He went to put on his Walkman to help kill some time, but damn it, he had left it at home.

Twenty minutes past his appointed time, Digger heard the clip-clopping of high-heeled footsteps approaching. A harried-looking woman came out and introduced herself.

"Hi. I'm Wendy and you must be Bugger." She offered her hand with her arm fully extended.

"Digger."

"Digger! Right! So sorry. Follow me."

After climbing two flights of stairs, Wendy gave Digger the lay of the land, the offices and where the restrooms and copy machines were.

He was then shown to a large conference room with a high ceiling and a wall of floor-to-ceiling windows that brought to mind King Arthur's Court. The long, shiny wooden table must have been custom-made and cost a fortune. Digger ran his flat hand along the rich grain before setting up his gear.

"This is where you'll be working. Dale, the director, is busy, wrapping something up. He should be in shortly. Grab yourself some coffee and Meg'll get you anything you need."

"Thanks."

Wendy clip-clopped out of the room on her heels and Meg entered. Meg was short and sturdy, wearing shredded jeans and a T-shirt with the hand stenciled logo for the band FEAR on it. She had a bleached, cropped punkish hairstyle.

Digger unpacked his kit and looked for an electrical outlet to plug in his pencil sharpener when he remembered that he was missing something.

"Oh, crap."

"What is it? Can I get you anything?" asked Meg.

"Oh, it's just that I forgot my Walkman."

"Can I help you with anything else?"

"No. I don't think so. Thanks anyway."

Meg disappeared and Digger continued to set up his aluminum briefcase easel and box of markers. He used an old cardboard beer bottle six-pack caddy for carrying markers. It was much better than anything in the art supply stores. It had a little handle and everything.

Meg returned with a boom box that played tapes and CDs. *CDs*! Plus a box filled with cassettes and compact discs.

"Here you go. I hope you find something in there you like."

"Wow! Where did you get this?" asked Digger.

"My office. Just call or come get me if you need anything else."

With that, Meg disappeared again.

Eventually, a man looking as young as Digger came in, wearing a Panavision cap, jeans, a white undershirt, and a dress shirt, unbuttoned and untucked.

"Hey, I'm Dale."

"Digger."

"You have a chance to read the script?"

"I haven't been given a script," Digger told him, feeling somehow guilty, as if it were his own fault.

"Oh, just great." Dale grabbed the nearby phone and punched a few buttons.

"Yeah, can we get two 'Bounce, Piggy!' trailer scripts over here in the conference room."

When the scripts came, Dale and Digger walked through them together.

"Now, these aren't just shooting boards, they're also to present to the client, so they have to be 'on model.' Get me?"

"Mickey Mouse has to look like Mickey Mouse."

"You got it. Knock it out of the park, rock star."

Dale left Digger to get started.

Digger boarded out the story beats in thumbnail form.

This wasn't a live-action spot. It was animation. Something else became more and more obvious to Digger.

Digger picked up the phone and dialed Dale's extension. Dale materialized immediately.

"What's up?"

"Dale, I gotta tell you something."

"Uh oh."

"I got good news and bad news. The bad news is you don't need me on this job. You need an animation guy. Those guys are a different breed. They draw completely differently. They have their own language. I could do this job but not nearly as well as an animation guy. They could do this in their sleep."

Dale closed his eyes and turned his chin to the ceiling. "Oh, god, make it stop."

"The good news is we still have time to call in an animation guy. I won't charge you a dime for me coming here, and you can have the thumbnails I did. I broke the whole script down."

Dale studied Digger.

"I like you. You have integrity. I think I'll stick with you. Do what you can. Finish out the day."

Dale went toward the kitchen and Digger put on one of Meg's Ramones CDs then fired up the pencil sharpener. He was gonna bust his ass to give this director his best.

Meg poked her head in.

"We're sending out for lattes. You want anything?"

Meg was back in a half hour, distributing coffee drinks to their rightful owners.

"How's it going?" asked Meg, handing him his iced tea.

"You tell me. I can't trust my eyes anymore." Digger pinched his eyes, rubbing them thoroughly.

Meg looked over the boards scattered on the mammoth conference table.

"These look good, but what do I know, right?" she confessed.

*

It was late at night. Digger had started at 4:00 pm.

Dale came in and grabbed a stack of the boards.

"Yeah," he said, smiling as he read the storyboards. "Yeah, these are great. I'm glad you decided to stay on."

Dale thanked Digger and Digger packed up his gear. Meg came in.

"Send me an invoice, yeah?"

"Will do. Thanks for the gig, Meg."

"Oh, anytime. It was our pleasure."

Before he left, Digger hit the copy machine. He got in the habit of making copies of all of his jobs and keeping them on file at home.

Digger yawned as he made the drive home. It was 1:15 am by the time he got there. He chuckled to think that in Spain, he'd just be getting to a nightclub. *Well, that was then and this is now.*

He wondered what the Téllez family was up to. He didn't leave on specifically *bad* terms, but they didn't exactly ask him to keep in touch.

For now, he was just grateful for his bed. He plowed into it. But, sleep did not come immediately.

Chapter 53 - Matinees at the Marina

The phone was quiet for the next few days. Digger caught up on some reading, walked on the boardwalk and practiced his ballroom steps.

He decided to catch a matinee in the marina. *Dirty Rotten Scoundrels* started in ten minutes. He bought a ticket and headed for the concession stand. It struck him to be an oxymoron, *concession stand*.

He sat there in the dark theater, chuckling as he threw popcorn and chocolate-covered almonds into his mouth, when his new pager went off. He had gotten it out of necessity, now that he was "in demand."

The pager display glowed in the dark, eliciting a "Hey, knock it off!" from the woman next to him.

It read "Hawkins Marsh 911."

It was Olivia.

Digger dropped everything and called from the lobby payphone.

"Hey, Dig. It's me, Clifford from Hawkins and Marsh. Can you come in tomorrow at, maybe 8:30, before most of the others? I got a special project for you. Top secret. Hush hush."

"Yeah, sure."

Digger went back into the theater. He hated that he had missed some of the movie.

When Digger reemerged into the outside world, he squinted and blinked at the harsh sunlight that washed all of the colors away.

He took the escalator down from the theater and walked past the shops and food joints toward the parking structure.

Digger felt a jolt. He stopped dead in his tracks.

There they were, sitting and having lunch, surrounded by shopping bags.

It was his estranged mother and sister Audrey. He hadn't spoken to either of them in three years, since he fled for Spain.

They looked up and saw him, also.

He considered leaving them with a nod, but his mother called out.

"Digger!"

He walked over to them, hating himself for not parking at a different lot.

"So, what are you two doing so far from home?" asked Digger, as if he hadn't completely disappeared on them.

"Some shopping. Your sister's getting married," his mother gloated. "Go on, show him the rock!"

Audrey also behaved as if this was all a normal interaction. She scoffed and reluctantly jammed her engagement ring into Digger's view. Her face still bore the expression of one enduring present company.

"Wonder where I've been?" asked Digger.

"We don't care, Digger," his mother answered, apparently speaking for his sister as well. "You left, so stay gone." She gave a fake smile. "If it's all the same to you."

"Audrey?" asked Digger.

Audrey looked Digger up and down. He was no longer her scruffy kid brother in torn jeans and a rock and roll T-shirt. No. He looked put together now.

"We're getting along fine without you, Digger," said Audrey, dead-faced. "You bailed."

Digger got a lump in his throat.

"You think you can just vanish like your goddamn old man and then it's suddenly, Hey everybody! Come kiss my ass because I *decided* to once again grace you with my presence? No thanks, pal." said Mother.

Digger just stood, trying to maintain his balance. "I guess I'll see you two around."

"Doubt it," added Audrey.

Digger walked away. He didn't head for his car. He walked to the marina, where he shuffled along the docks and piers, his mind a complete blank. He was in shock, having free-fallen from all sensation.

Despite all of the years of abuse at the hands of his mother, this hurt. It was worse than all of the bloody noses and hateful dress-downs.

What really surprised him was Audrey. Maybe it shouldn't have.

Tears welled up in his eyes. *I'm her only son,* he thought. *Did you look for me, mother? I would have.*

Chapter 54 - Top Secret

Riding the elevator up, Digger had a weird feeling about this one. It was 8:15, fifteen minutes before the time Clifford had asked him to show up.

He got off on the sixth floor at Hawkins and Marsh and headed for reception. That was when Clifford intercepted him.

"Great! You're early!"

Clifford whisked Digger into an empty office in the far corner of the floor rather frantically, as if trying to hide a mistress.

Once inside, Digger set his work kit down and took a seat, cautiously.

"This one is just you and me, amigo. These boards are for an idea I want to pitch. These are presentation boards, not shooting boards, so they'll have to look real pretty, understand? No arrows. No captions. Take your time with these."

"So, no director?" Digger looked around and saw the half-sheets of Blackcore foam mounting boards and Super 77 aerosol spray adhesive, X-Acto knives—stuff one would need for mounting and presenting concept art.

"Just think of me as the director. Yes! *I* am the director. Bathroom's right across from you. I'll bring your lunch. Whatever you want. So, you don't really have to go anywhere."

"Uh, whatever you say."

"Well, I say *stay put*."

This all sounded *muy suspicioso* to Digger.

They got down to business. Clifford was not an articulate client.

"No, no, no. This is all wrong! The koala's got the *blues*! This isn't what I have in mind!"

"No, Clifford. The boards are not *wrong*. They just require *revision*. This is part of the process. I'm following the script you gave me. You want to change the script? Fine. But don't blame me because you're changing your script. Just take a breath."

Clifford seemed to settle a little somewhat. "You're right. I need lunch. I'll be right back with some take-out menus."

Digger kept working. He couldn't read Clifford's mind, but he knew how to tell a solid story. Anyone presenting *these* boards would *not* look like a fool.

*

After lunch (chicken curry!), Olivia popped her head in unexpectedly.

"So, it's you! I'd wondered who they'd stuck in here."

Olivia perused Digger's handiwork and the mounting materials around him.

"Mounting's done in the graphics and production room," she said to no one in particular, in a tone that closely resembled scolding.

She left the room briefly, returning with Clifford in tow.

"Clifford. What the fuck is this?"

"It's just a project that you're not involved with. That's all."

"Not involved with? That's all? Clifford, who is this for?"

"It's for Koala Blue."

"You're pitching to Koala Blue behind Hawkins and Marsh's back? Using their money?!"

"Look. Olivia. Please."

"See here, Clifford. I will not turn you in to the higher-ups, but when you pitch this, the account goes to Hawkins and Marsh. Understood?"

"Understood."

Olivia left the tiny office. Clifford looked to Digger. Digger's mind chewed on thoughts about Clifford. Clifford was a crook. Beside that, he was scary.

"It's always a woman, innit? They always have to screw up everything, don't they?"

Digger didn't furnish a response.

"Yeah. You always keep your mouth shut. I guess you're the smart one."

Chapter 55 - Clive

Clive hoofed it through the Malaysian jungle away from the Jeep, following an entourage and tailed by an interpreter. With each branch that thrashed or whacked his face, he considered tendering his resignation.

High in the mountains, they reached a clearing. Now, they could hike and crawl up the rocks to get a better view of the region.

"You," commanded Clive, "Tell the owner that we wish to buy the property that my employer and he had discussed." Clive waited for the translation before continuing. "But your survey lines are wrong."

On cue, the translator produced satellite maps from long plastic tubes, carried with straps like quivers full of arrows, and handed them to Clive.

"This property you wish to sell us does not extend to the line you had furnished us. It extends—" Clive searched the maps for the proper one, then pointed, "only to this one. This whole skirt of land around the proposed sale belongs to someone else. You are trying to sell us the whole egg when you only own the yolk." The translator relayed this to the owner.

This latest message seemed to upset the owner as he shouted something in Malaysian which sent the property owner's men shaking their rifles and *parang* (machetes) at Clive.

"In fact. You have been selling," Clive pulled out map after map, "quite a few eggs, haven't you, Harun?"

Clive was unfazed by the weapons trained upon him. "Okay Harun. The price I'm gonna offer you is so low that you will consider it a mortal insult, and you'll take it."

Harun's shocked expression caused his men to jump.

His grunts took low aim at Clive. A *keris* (knife) was pressed to his neck.

"And if anything happens to me, my employer will have you audited and investigated for the last six land sales to American businessmen that you have made. I think you know that my employer is good friends with His Royal Highness, the King."

The radio crackled to life. A call had been relayed. It was Bobby's father.

Clive listened and he nodded. Silently he raised his foot crotch high and stomped it into the mud in frustration. "Yessir. Right away, Sir," were the only words he spoke. After the call ended, he spat and swore as he handed the radio handset back to its operator. Clive waved both arms above his head, as if trying to signal a helicopter. It was off. The whole thing was off.

*

Clive thanked the Gods for strong water pressure and a working hot water heater as he melted in the hotel shower. His every muscle punished him for the past three days—days without sleep, days without real food and without a break. Days with bugs.

The hotel phone rang.

"Are you kidding me? I'm taking a goddamn shower!" Clive yelled into the shower head.

Still sopping wet, Clive wrapped his waist in a towel and dripped his way to the phone. He had a broad chest, protected by a healthy coat of body hair. He looked like the Texaco Man.

"Yeah?" Clive yelled. The phone was staticky. It sounded like a long distance call.

It was Robert Sr. the head of the wealthy Werner family.

"Yeah, yeah. I can be there. It'll take me a couple of days. What's this all about?"

Of course. It's about Bobby. Always Bobby. Pain in the ass Bobby.

The only good reason for Clive to see Bobby was to deliver a military-grade spanking.

*

A day and a half later, a private car delivered Clive to a mansion in the Malibu hills, where he was to hold a private audience with Robert Sr. and his son, Bobby. This was a big deal. Clive would not have been called if it weren't.

Clive was clean-shaven and pressed. Half a bottle of Visine brought his eyes back to pink. His hair was slick and tight.

"No more! No more of your art buying! You pay too much and don't even authenticate properly!" yelled the wealthy patriarch to his embarrassed middle-aged son.

"Sir, if I may," began Clive. "I could run a comb through Bobby's entire collection, starting with the Picasso and Matisses. Then we could have them properly insured."

"No! My stuff is nobody else's business!"

"Some of your pieces are stolen, aren't they, Bobby?" asked his father.

"It's my stuff," declared a defiant Bobby Jr. "And nobody's touching it."

Chapter 56 - I Like You

It was overcast on Laurie's day off. She had taken Digger's hand at the matinee, *Miracle Mile*. *Tonight, I'll make him dinner*. The thought of it made her laugh. *Dinner for Digger*.

In her bedroom, just after sex, Laurie rolled over and turned the sound down on the small boom box on the floor next to the bed.

"I like you, Digger."

"I like you, too, Laurie," Digger replied, staring at the ceiling.

"No, not like that. I really like you. Do you like me, too?"

Digger sat up. "Laurie. What is the answer you're fishing for?"

"You're supposed to say, I love you, you asshole."

Digger sat silent for a moment. He felt like he was about to attempt to disarm a bomb.

"I'm sorry that I don't have that answer for you, but that doesn't make me an asshole. Other things make me an asshole."

"Don't try being funny, asshole. Get out."

"You're sure you don't want to talk about this? We do like each other after all."

"Out!"

Digger grabbed his underwear, pants and shoes and took them to the living room to dress. He was fully clothed when he returned to the bedroom doorway.

Laurie was staring at a poster of Hello Kitty on her wall.

"You're sure you're okay?" queried Digger.

"Out."

Digger left her looking hurt and confused.

*

Later that night, Digger's phone rang. It was Laurie. What a relief. He knew it would have been no use calling her to talk. It had to be when *she* was ready.

"Digger?"

"Yes, Laurie?"

"I'm late," she said. "I'm late and I won't take a life, Digger."

"Hold on."

"I'm pregnant, Digger."

"I'm coming right over."

"No!"

But it was too late. Digger was on his way. He drove over to Laurie's place.

Digger entered through the open front door of her small rental house.

Laurie was in the kitchen, next to the mustard-colored phone. She was tapping it with her forefinger, absently. She flinched when she saw Digger in the doorway. "You startled me."

"May I come in and sit down?"

"You're already in, asshole."

"Can we dispense with the pet names for the time being?"

They discussed home pregnancy tests, menstrual calendars and the prospect of being unexpected parents. Suddenly, she reversed course.

"I can take care of it. I'll need a thousand dollars."

"Nothing doing." Although a thousand dollars was more than a bargain to not be in this situation, that would not really solve this particular problem. "You're not being straight with me."

"Why aren't you scared? Why aren't you crying?!" Laurie screamed at him. "You're scary, Digger. Your stare scares me. You have the calm of someone capable of literally anything."

Digger could not come up with a response to a statement like that.

They sat for what felt like hours. He told her that he would support anything she decided.

When she finally spoke, it was without drama, as if they had been spending the evening making small talk. She finally confessed.

"There is no pregnancy. I was just so hurt about your not having the same feelings for me. That's all."

Digger left. By whose decision was anybody's guess.

*

Digger's phone rang. It had to be Laurie, calling from who knows where.

"Hello?"

"Digger, it's Olivia." This took him aback for a moment. "More storyboards?"

"No. I was just calling to say hi. Didn't see you at ballroom last Thursday."

Digger didn't furnish an alibi. "So, Olivia. How's tricks?"

"Tricks is good," she said. "Say, I know it's a little late, but have you eaten?"

"Nope," Digger lied.

*

They met at a bar and grille on the ground floor of the building where she worked on Wilshire Blvd. Digger wore an indigo silk shirt and black slacks. He caught a head-to-toe glimpse of himself in a reflective surface as he approached the front door. *Sharp.*

When he entered, the hostess asked him about his "party" and he just looked around the room until he spotted Olivia sitting at the bar. She picked up her glass of wine and small plate of fried brie and motioned Digger toward one of the booths that ran along the wall.

The hostess followed along, grabbing a couple of menus before telling Digger, "Right this way."

The hostess seated Digger, who got there just after Olivia.

"So, *Digger*, you never did storyboards before and then, Bam! all of a sudden, you've dropped everything to do storyboards for Hawkins and Marsh—"

"Among others."

"Among others. That's right. And you attend ballroom dancing classes without being dragged by a wife, or fianceé, or girlfriend. Just who are you, Mr. Digger?"

"What do you want to know?"

"First of all, don't lie to me. Don't ever lie to me. Got it?"

"Got it."

"What were you doing right, I mean, right before I met you and you turned into Super Storyboard Man?"

"I was bumming around Europe," he said.

"Oh, my god! That sounds fabulous." Olivia sipped her red wine.

"You been?" Digger asked.

"Only Paris," said Olivia, silently offering Digger a piece of brie and bread.

"Paris is good," said Digger, taking a piece of the brie.

"Paris is good? Come on, man. Paris is fucking great!" She leaned back into a heavy sigh.

"So, Digger. Why does everybody call you that?"

"Because I answer when they do," Digger flirted.

"Fair enough. You got a girlfriend? Digger?"

"Who's asking?"

"I am, Digger." Olivia looked Digger square in the eyes. "I am."

Chapter 57 - Days and Nights in Love

Digger and Olivia began a light and breezy relationship. They talked all night on the phone. "Don'tcha hate this?" "Don'tcha love that?" They spoke of nothing. They talked about everything. They talked about art. They talked about books and language. They talked about music, math and model systems. The one thing they didn't speak about was their pasts.

The sun was coming up by the time they said their good nights.

The next day, Digger met Olivia at the box office for the 1:30 pm showing of *Cinema Paradiso*. They each had slept in after the long night before and couldn't stop grinning at each other.

After the coming attractions and well into the feature, Olivia took Digger's hand, intertwining their fingers. Minutes later, as they watched the movie screen, she began to kiss the back of Digger's hand, lightly, sweetly. Soon, Digger brought their clasped hands to his lips, kissing the back of Olivia's hand. Keeping her eyes forward was becoming increasingly difficult. He kept his eyes forward also. She then took his thumb into her mouth and slid it back and forth, raking her teeth along its fleshy side. Digger then took each of her fingers, one at a time, and slurped them, slowly, repeatedly.

They never took their eyes off the screen.

Olivia scooted down in her seat and nestled her head into Digger's neck.

The movie was good. The date was magic.

Chapter 58 - Clifford Taught Me

Olivia and Digger sat on her sofa after making out. Olivia picked up the remote and turned the TV off.

Her apartment had style. Nothing over the top. Nothing "tacky." It had peach walls with white trim.

"I like your place. Comfy," observed Digger.

"Well, I'm glad." She grinned at him cozily. "Digger, I've been thinking. You hardly spend anything. What do you do with all of your storyboard money?"

"A gentleman never tells." Digger turned mischievous. "I spend it all on birthday presents!" Digger soft tackled Olivia. "No, seriously. I just sock it away, I guess."

"You need to make your money work for you, Digger."

"Are you gonna sell me a timeshare?"

Olivia laughed. "Sign here! No, but I think you should give some thought to playing the market."

"The stock market?"

"No, the fish market. You're smart, and better yet, you're not stupid. A lot of smart people lose their shirts 'cause they get stupid."

"I don't know anything about the stock market."

"I do. I'll show you." Olivia grabbed the newspaper off her coffee table. "It's not hard so long as you only play what you know and don't get cocky. It's a big ocean out there. You can drown."

"What's the worst-case scenario?"

"You lose your money."

"Okay, I'm in."

"It's easy. Clifford taught me."

"Clifford?" Digger could not mask his disbelief.

"Hey, hey. Be nice to me. Remember, I've got a birthday coming up." This was true. She had mentioned that to him earlier. Her birthday was July 7th, roughly a month after Digger's, although he never mentioned it. It was just one of the many things he preferred not to discuss. There were many things about himself he would have rather not have discussed, things he felt were going to come out anyway.

Chapter 59 - Clifford Finds Out

Digger was to do boards for another team at Hawkins and Marsh, Deirdre's team. It would be on location in a production trailer in downtown LA. He showed up at the skyscraper-lined street at 7:30 am with his work kit(s) in tow.

The dozens of trailers were lined up single file along both sides of the street, blocking off all traffic. There were electrical cords tangled all over the concrete.

He'd been briefed that the director was storyboarding one commercial while shooting another. Digger would be working with a famous English feature film director who had made only one film for the American market. Commercials were just in-between side gigs.

When Digger arrived, the exasperated director introduced himself.

"Hello, I'm Tony."

"Digger."

"Digger, can you draw ducks like Francis Bacon?"

Digger thought about this quickly but thoroughly. "Yes. Why, yes. I can."

Tony had a cool shaved head and industrial-style eyeglass frames that looked expensive. Digger wanted to tell Tony how much he loved his movie, but thought better of it. This was a time for work. He had no business jeopardizing a smooth gig by acting starstruck.

They chatted for a bit.

"Finally, I've found someone I can work with! No offense but, I find most American storyboard artists ignorant and slow."

"No offense taken. I seem to have that problem with many people."

"So, Digger what do you like to draw when you're not drawing storyboards?"

"Not much, really. I've pretty much given up recreational drawing, for the time being anyway. All the drawing I do lately is for advertising boards. No more sketchbooks either, really."

"I want to say that's a shame but, hell, if you don't feel like it, don't do it," Tony commented. "But, it is a shame."

They sat down in the cramped space at a fold-out table inside the trailer. Digger sketched on a pad of tracing paper as Tony acted out scene after scene, gesticulating with great flourish.

It was a spot for a dishwashing liquid. It was a campaign that centered on the efforts to use only this liquid detergent to remove the oil from water birds after a devastating oil spill. When Tony felt that Digger had been sufficiently briefed, he left the trailer to put out the fires that directors put out.

Digger stared at his blank page. Tony had shown him footage of the oil spill rescue efforts, how they sprayed and hosed and gently scrubbed the ducks, some sedate and surrendering, some flapping their wings in fear. Digger then drew the story— Ducks on the shore, covered in goo. Nice people scooping up the ducks. Shot of the product, the liquid soap. Gloved hands cleaning the ducks. Then the freed ducks flapping away. No sweat. His pencil flew in slashing strokes, emulating the ghostly motion found in Bacon's paintings.

A few hours later, a producer poked her head in and told Digger to break for lunch and he set out to find a decent-sized bathroom. He left the trailer and its tiny bathroom and walked out onto the street surrounded by a canyon of skyscrapers. He trotted with a sense of urgency. He really needed that bathroom.

Digger entered a business building lobby and hunted for clues. He asked a couple of passers-by but they just shrugged. "Can't help ya' pal," said one.

Finally, Digger found an Udon fast-food place. He inquired about the "facilities" and was told "customers only." He power-walked straight for the men's room.

When he was finished, he walked, ever so relieved, over to the counter to put in an order.

As he placed his tray on the table, he wished he were having lunch with Tony. He liked Tony and liked working with him. Tony actually put words together, not just stock phrases linked by the word "like." Tony was smart and made smart jokes.

Digger liked that this place served fresh ginger on the side.

When he finished his meal, Digger went back to the trailer to finish out the long day.

Tony was thrilled with Digger's work. Digger didn't ask but secretly hoped that they would work together again.

Later the same day, Digger came into the Hawkins and Marsh offices to drop off some invoices. It was well past quitting time. He was asked to wait for Deidre in the glass-encased conference room.

Olivia popped into the room and kissed Digger on the cheek when nobody appeared to be watching. She looked a little run-down.

"Hey stranger. See you at home."

"Where's home?" asked Digger.

"Your place."

"Then, you bet."

"I will be late though," Olivia explained. "You know how it is."

"Yeah, I know. Don't burn yourself out now. You look a little pale."

"I have a UTI."

"Oh, baby," Digger said, soothingly.

Clifford was watching the entire time.

*

Ready to go home, Olivia entered Clifford's office holding a sheaf of papers. Her breathing was a tad labored.

His office had no real evidence of a personality. No guitar, no trophies, no photos —Olivia had taken back the single photo he had on his desk. It was of the two of them wearing Christmas sweaters bonking their heads together— no golf clubs. There was only a framed "motivational" poster on the wall of some birch trees that read, "SUCCESS."

"Hey, Clifford. Do you know anything about these? They're purchase orders for a bunch of stuff, namely art supplies. This is way beyond what accounting says is normal."

Clifford looked over the purchase orders. "Yeah, you signed for these. See? Your initials."

"First of all, I don't initial POs, I sign them. Second of all, where's all of the inventory? I just checked the office supply room and it's pretty bare bones."

"Just chalk it up to employee theft," Clifford shrugged.

"Employee theft? You think our guys are stealing—" she consulted the POs, "dozens of airbrushes, air compressors, entire designer marker sets…"

"What about the freelancers?"

"Freelancers? You mean Digger. Oh, Clifford. What is wrong with you?"

"With me?"

"You're behind this, aren't you?" accused Olivia.

"Don't you go spreading rumors about anyone, Olivia."

"Isn't that your schtick, Clifford?"

"Who? Me?" said Clifford in mock offense. "Olivia, you okay? You're looking a little sluggish." He placed the back of his hand on her forehead. "A bit clammy."

"Don't get smart, Clifford. I know about some of the skeletons in your closet."

"It would be a shame if no one could trust your little friend anymore, Olivia. By the way, you can prove… nothing."

"And Clifford, I want to know your plan for getting my money back to me."

"Plan?" Clifford smiled. "No plan."

Chapter 60 - Olivia Goes Down

Digger saw that a Georgia O'Keeffe show was opening at LACMA (the Los Angeles County Museum of Art) on Friday evening in the Weekly. Olivia said that it sounded like fun so there they went.

The mixer that accompanied the opening of the show took place in the main gallery. People bent at the waist, forward, then backward, staring and squinting at the watercolor renderings of swirling desert storms and exploding flowers, while sipping their sparkling wines.

Digger and Olivia were smartly dressed. They spoke to each other in hushed tones as they took in the paintings, refuting the oft-repeated notion that O'Keeffe's flowers were solid representations of the vagina.

He recognized a few faces from Design Center and from the galas and soirees he'd attended years ago with Beverly, patrons of the arts, aficionados, artists and students. One of those faces he recognized made him stop. It gave him chills. He would remember that face anywhere. It was Melman.

It was pompous, bearded and beady-eyed Melman, who had authenticated the counterfeit Matisse drawings that Digger had sold to the wealthy eccentric Bobby Werner Jr. three years ago.

Melman was holding court, surrounded by those who did and did not know of him.

"Yes, I had the good fortune to dine with Ms. O'Keeffe in 1985," Melman bellowed. "Say! That was the very same

248

year that I had the good fortune to acquire a couple of fine original drawings by one Henri Matisse!"

Digger's skin pimpled. His blood froze.

This bit of social gossip caused the immediate crowd to stir.

It was while he was blowing smoke about O'Keeffe that his gaze met Digger's.

"You. Don't I know you?" asked Melman.

Digger rushed to confirm that they had once met at an LA soiree and not in Chicago, that Digger was not the Italian young man who had furnished the secret Matisses. *These aren't the droids you're looking for.*

No, Melman had no clue that it was Digger who, in disguise, had conned him into authenticating fake Matisses in haste, so that he could satisfy his lust to take two for himself.

That was three years ago.

"Well, we must be going now, Mr. Melman. *Arriverderci!*" said a cheeky Digger, reviving the Italian accent he had used during the art swap con job.

Melman complimented him on his accent as he and Olivia disappeared into the crowd.

Digger looked at Olivia. She was pale. She looked weak. She had been running herself down.

"Olivia? Are you okay?"

She slumped, then collapsed to the floor.

Chapter 61- Sepsis

The paramedics finally showed up. They hopped out of their ambulance van with less urgency than on TV. They swarmed around Olivia without facing her. They popped open big kits filled with blood pressure cuffs, tubes, bandages and stethoscopes. This was just another stop to them.

Digger was anxious to get Olivia to the hospital, but the EMTs kept telling him to calm down. They took her blood pressure and listened to her breathing. They talked to each other as if they were alone in a locker room.

Olivia rocked back and forth. "I feel like I'm being sawed in half."

"She looks fine. Breathing, fine. Blood pressure's a little on the low end of normal," said an EMT.

"I have a history of sepsis," said Olivia. "My kidneys hurt."

"You look fine. You sound fine. You don't look septic," the EMT insisted.

"Insist, Olivia," urged Digger.

"Take me to a hospital."

The EMT scoffed, but complied.

Digger followed the ambulance in his car. The EMTs wouldn't let him ride in the ambulance because he wasn't family.

The two EMTs bantered loudly about their weekend plans, laughing as they took Olivia out of the ambulance and wheeled her into the hospital and down the hall on a gurney. Digger tailed them closely, feeling alert and concerned.

They made a few turns and then parked her in a hallway.

"You, wait right here," ordered the taller EMT.

"Like, where were we gonna go?" said Digger in a soft voice to Olivia. She let out a small, yet painful, grin.

Digger held Olivia's hand and she squeezed it hard periodically, seized by pain.

She moaned deeply.

"You're gonna be alright. I'm here, doll. Squeeze my hand."

She did.

Damn! She's strong. He thought she might break his bones.

The EMTs returned and released the foot brake on the gurney.

"Got a room for you. Taking you there right now. Just relax."

They rolled her to the ER.

When the EMTs and nurses stuffed Olivia into the room, it was like a scene from the Marx Brothers. The six people in that tiny room accentuated how small the room actually was.

Olivia was oriented facing the clock on the wall, with a stack of beeping machines on her right, between her and the door. The crowd bled out of the room.

Another person in scrubs materialized and gave Digger a clipboard with some forms and a pen, then disappeared.

Olivia clutched her gut as another wave of pain crested inside of her. Digger took up the clipboard and pen and began to fill out the paperwork, taking dictation from Olivia between convulsions. He filled in her name, address, social security number and other pertinent information.

They waited for quite a while, maybe forty-five minutes. Each of Olivia's convulsions seized Digger, squeezed him, shook him.

Where the hell was the doctor? A nurse?

Just then, a nurse burst through the curtains.

"Doctor will be right with you. Have you filled out the forms?"

"I believe so." Digger said, handing over the clipboard.

"What is your insurance?" asked the nurse, tapping the clipboard with the pen.

Digger answered without a moment's thought.

"That'll be cash."

"Cash? You're gonna have to set something up with finance right away. They'll likely need some sort of deposit—"

"I'll talk to finance," Digger said, with a touch of menace in his voice.

After a battery of medical questions, the nurse left the room.

"Digger. What are you doing? I have insurance. I can't pay cash."

Olivia convulsed again, this time emitting a deep cry. Not loud, but heartbreaking. It was a brave sound, the sound of pain leaking out of her tremendous strength. It crushed Digger somewhere inside of his ribs.

A bespectacled man wearing a white coat and stethoscope opened the door and entered.

"Hi there. I'm Dr. Ikehara. So, what's going on today?"

"I think it's sepsis. I've had it before." Olivia sounded deceptively lucid between eruptions. It was misleading to be sure. People didn't believe that you were sick when you could articulate your experience, in the same way that they don't believe your innocence unless you can argue it on the witness stand.

"Sepsis?" the doctor repeated as if Olivia were trying to get out of gym class, "Well, we'll see about that." He turned to Digger.

"And you are family—?"

"Yes," Olivia interrupted.

After more condescending talk, Dr. Ikehara left.

One of the interchangeable nurses returned.

"Doctor ordered tests for you."

"I haven't eaten for quite a bit. I'm hungry. And, could I get some water?" asked a weakened Olivia.

"Doctor said, no food or liquids until the labs come back."

"Not even water?" joined Digger.

The nurse shook her head. Digger tried to get a look at the name on her lanyard, but it was facing the wrong way. The nurse left.

"I'm gonna get you some food and water."

"But, Digger the nurse said—"

"By the time we get the a-okay, you'll be passing out. This way, we won't have to go hunting when we do get the green light. I'll be right back." He kissed her on the temple. "I promise."

Digger made his way through the halls like a mouse in a maze.

He found a nurses' station. People in scrubs were shooting the shit like they had nothing better to do.

"Excuse me? Where could I get some food?"

"The cafeteria," said one without looking at Digger.

Another pointed down the hall straight ahead. He went down the hall.

Yet another person sent him up an elevator. There, he went.

He asked a couple more people in the corridors until he hit a sign with a useful arrow.

Digger finally reached the cafeteria. It was your standard tile and stainless affair with a couple of vending machines thrown in for good measure. With the harsh fluorescent lighting, one would think it was a surgical theater. The menu had black and red push-in plastic letters. He took a plastic tray from the stack and slid it along the long metal shelf.

There were soups, today's being split pea and chicken noodle. The cafeteria also offered pizza bagels, pre-wrapped sandwiches and fresh fruit. There was also today's special: veggie lasagna.

He figured the sandwiches were probably the least messy option, so he opted for a couple of those—turkey and roast beef—and a couple of apple juices.

Digger slid his tray to the cashier who took nearly eight dollars (!) from him.

They thanked each other and Digger set off, trying to remember exactly how to get back to Olivia's room.

On his way back, Digger saw the ER explode into action and he felt a flash of panic.

Folks in scrubs all scurried frantically, many swarming around a gurney that was being rushed in. The patient on the gurney was in a complex contraption like the one holding his head immobile.

"What's going on?" Digger asked the general flurry.

"Motorcycle accident," somebody said.

Digger took his food tray and headed for Olivia's room, dodging a couple of interns on the way.

When Digger entered Olivia's room, she was wet with perspiration. *She must be going through hell.*

"Go ahead and eat, Digger. The nurse hasn't come back yet."

"Nothing doin.' I eat when you eat. Any word?"

Olivia shook her head, no.

Finally the doctor came back. He let out a big breath.

"Just as I thought. Sepsis. It's bad," said Dr. Ikehara.

Just as I thought? thought Digger. *We told* you*, you prick.* Digger really hated this doctor.

"We're going to admit you, get you started right away on IV antibiotics."

"How bad is it?" asked Olivia.

The doctor looked at Digger.

"Whatever you have to say, Doctor, you can say in front of him."

"The infection is bone deep," began the doctor, bracing himself. "Just in case, you might want to get your affairs in order."

Chapter 62 - Help Me

Olivia just may die.

Digger had to face this thought, and facing it shook all pride from him. He didn't care what he looked like, what anyone thought of him... If there were a higher power, he'd readily submit.

He drove the freeways until he felt it unsafe to do so. Digger was a trembling mess.

Olivia was his first love. First in the way of spine-tingling kisses. First in the way of caring about someone beyond caring about oneself.

Although he had lived life before he met her, it wasn't a full life. How could he go on? He was frozen with befuddlement.

It was his way to look at the worst-case scenario and be grateful that it never got as bad as all that. But this was different. Digger seemed to have no choice in what perspective to take. This wasn't a game.

He had wanted to stay longer at the hospital, but Olivia needed her rest and his presence obviously sapped her strength, expending energy she didn't have in order to be pleasant company.

Digger entered his bungalow house and sat at the dining room table with the lights off. There he would remain all night.

*

Impressing her doctors, Olivia was still in the hospital after three weeks, bucking in pain, having IV antibiotics pumped into her around the clock. But, she was still alive.

To ask her, the sensation was like being boiled in oil and feeling each cell scream.

Digger visited nearly every day, all day long. Sometimes, the nurses looked the other way and he slept overnight in the padded chair with a hospital blanket.

Olivia was weak, too weak for anger or self-pity. Pain had wrung her out.

One night, while Digger was away, she wiggled herself until she fell out of the bed.

Out of her mind with pain and dripping with sweat, she crawled on her belly, out of her room and down the hall to the nurses' station. When they saw her, she reached out for them and croaked, in a voice feeble with weakness, "Help me."

Chapter 63 - Fresh T-Shirts

About a week later, Olivia had turned a corner. She no longer appeared to be a terminal case. She merely looked… sick.

Digger placed the tote bag into the closet full of gowns and bedding. "I brought you some fresh t-shirts. I know how much you hate hospital gowns."

"Digger. I just can't just lie here. I am missing so much work." She still sounded feeble.

"I don't think you have much of a choice," Digger laughed, "Although, it's good to see you looking strong enough to argue." He pulled the chair close to Olivia's bed and sat. "Is it the money? Don't worry about anything, Olivia. Everything will all work out."

"What, are you some kind of drug dealer? What's with all this cash and no job?"

"No. I'm an earner and a saver."

"I'll say." Olivia squirmed in a flash of pain. Digger winced.

"Besides, I have a job now," Digger gave a little smile. "Thanks to you."

"You know how short-staffed we are, Digger. I can't leave Clifford to his own devices. He drives people away," she continued.

"Why don't they just *fire* him?"

"The owners just love Clifford. He really knows how to lay it on thick. He's a genius ass-kisser."

"Well, it worked on you."

"What is that supposed to mean?"

"I'm just noting that you once fell for whatever he passes for charm. I mean, you *were* and item once."

"I didn't *fall* for—" She turned away from Digger. "Never mind."

"Oh, Olivia. I'm sorry."

"Digger, could you go home now?"

Digger slowly got up from the chair and looked at Olivia, as if to ask, *Are you sure?*

After he got his silent answer, he left Olivia's room.

Chapter 64 - Time Collapses

The TV in her hospital room was off. The only movement came from the hands of the wall clock. Time expanded and collapsed for Olivia. She could not tell an hour from a minute. She closed her eyes and focused on her breathing, just like she learned in a meditation workshop in college. In, and out. In, and out.

Usually, a circumstance like this would induce boredom, but pain changed everything.

They say what doesn't kill you makes you stronger. What a short-sighted thing to say. Pain, over time, warps your very soul. In, and out.

There was a knock at the door.

Oh, for Christ's sake. They're here to draw more blood.

The large door creaked open, but Olivia could not see who it was. Could it be Digger? Here to offer a second, reinforcing apology? She half-hoped it was.

The privacy curtain moved aside. It was Clifford. He brought flowers.

"I can't stay long. The nurses said that visiting hours are almost over." Clifford didn't sit. "One of them gave me this." He produced a cheap textured glass vase. "I think it might've been from lost and found." Clifford put his bouquet into the vase and took it to the sink.

"Thanks, Clifford," Olivia said, a little softer than she had intended.

"So, how's the food?" he joked, running the water.

"They said I could die."

"Oh, that's just doctor talk." Clifford filled the vase halfway and then put it on her hospital table.

"What's going on at Hawkins and Marsh?"

"Without you there? It's the fall of Rome! Our pal, the director's panicked. Thinks he'll never work again. It's not just you. The guy has no people skills and his directing skills really aren't great enough to overlook that. He should be okay, though, once you come back. Things are pretty good otherwise. The agency got a couple of juicy new accounts, that went to other teams, of course."

"Of course."

Olivia jammed the call button. It had been forever since her last dose of morphine and she was feeling that all-over ache. She contorted in agitation,

Clifford asked, "Want me to fetch a nurse?"

Clifford disappeared behind the curtain. He returned, it seemed two weeks later, with the charge nurse.

"You're not due for another dose for another half hour, but it's near bedtime and your boyfriend here is so handsome." The charge nurse looked at Clifford as though he were covered in maple syrup.

"Not my—" stuttered Olivia.

The charge nurse took a syringe and got the needle into Olivia's IV catheter. She pressed the plunger and Olivia grimaced slightly at the cold shooting into her arm.

A few moments later, Olivia felt that buttery hug, that warm blizzard, swaddling her. She dropped straight out of this room, out of this moment and away from the pain.

"I think this is where I make my exit," Clifford announced to the charge nurse and what remained of Olivia.

Chapter 65 - Cold on the Outside

Digger sat at the counter at Norm's, sketching out ideas for Olivia's birthday card in his sketchbook. They had been on the outs for only a couple of days, but that was enough for Digger.

He was sliding all over the ice with no skates. He felt like he could take only so much more of this. First, Digger had been terrified of losing Olivia to sepsis. Now, he was faced with losing her again, this time over a stupid remark.

Digger decided to do something, something altogether non-LA. He went for a walk.

He headed down Lincoln Blvd. to Santa Monica Blvd., took a left and went down toward the beach to the mall.

His head bobbed along the flowing nighttime crowd of shoppers and sightseers. Digger looked at the window displays of the shops that sold clothing, toys, furniture, books and gourmet snacks.

He saw women, beautiful women. Although truth be told, Digger discovered that when he was drawing regularly he found most everybody attractive. Each face, each nose, each ear was pleasing and nourishing to his eye. Old men, young children, he could not look at a face without planning out how he would draw or paint them. Each one was a portrait waiting to happen.

He saw female bodies that whet his appetites. But, the longer he stayed with Olivia, the more his violent ideation subsided. Olivia made the world safer. Not safe, but safer.

Something in a storefront window brought him to a halt. He went in.

The place was a wonderland of replicas ranging from the late 1800s to the late 1970s. There were vintage-looking tins of Cracker Jack popcorn candy, Coca-Cola trays and 50s looking space ray guns. The spinning postcard rack was a special treat. Some postcards had all sorts of vintage advertisements and war posters, as well as old time celebrities like W.C. Fields and Mae West. Digger plucked a couple of Little Rascals cards from it and moved on. A wooden rack with two rows of large glass jars displayed stick candy that were striped like barber shop poles.

On his way to the register with his purchases, Digger spied a troll doll with orange hair. It was the goofiest thing he'd ever seen. It was dressed in a tiny, felt caveman (cavewoman?) tunic and had huge, gooey eyes. Of course, he bought it.

Digger entered a stationery store that had a modest art supply section where he found a smallish sheet of handmade paper, an envelope and a small watercolor kit.

Back home, Digger sat in his kitchenette with the door open and put on the radio. KROQ FM was playing Talking Heads' *Nothing But Flowers*. He took out a piece of heavy paper, one with some tooth to it, and folded it precisely in half. Digger tapped his Pentel plastic fountain pen absently, trying to think of something to lay down. The cats outside were on the roof except for one who rolled around on the walkway that led to his open back door.

Digger gave a silent *aha* and set his pen in motion. He drew a kitty like the one on his pathway in simple, clean line.

He stared at it for a moment before adding a bouquet of balloons, held in the cat's paw. *There. That's it.*

He opened the folded card and thought about the Happy Birthday message he would write inside. He considered including an apology in it.

No. He didn't want Olivia looking at this card, years in the future, and focusing on their spat. He finally wrote:

"Happy Birthday Olivia. Nothing makes any sense without you.

-Digger"

Digger laid the card flat, art side up, and sat there, allowing the ink to dry a little. He then got up and filled a plastic cup with water and brought some paper towels back to the table.

Digger tested the watercolor by brushing some color over just a small ink detail in the corner. Great! The ink line didn't smear.

Digger used the paintbrush to tint the balloon-bearing kitty in delicate washes.

When he was finished, Digger admired his handiwork. He liked what he saw and lingered over it. *Very Japanese*, he thought. The phone rang. He answered.

It was Olivia. Digger tensed up, both relieved and afraid. She consented to a visit.

*

When he got to the hospital, Olivia appeared surprisingly well. She had some real color in her face and seemed without anguish. She was sitting up and looked amazing without make-up.

Digger scooted the chair closer to her bed.

"Happy Birthday, Olivia," he said, handing her the card and wrapped gift.

"You know my birthday isn't for another ten days."

Digger shrugged.

She tore through the wrapping paper eagerly. Her excitement was short-lived. "Digger, this is the dumbest gift I've ever gotten in my life."

He looked at her expectantly.

"I love it," she said.

"Are we good?"

"Better than good. Now, let me see this card of yours."

Olivia read the card and tears welled up in her eyes. She motioned for Digger and he came in for an embrace.

"Digger, you mean so much to me. I want out of here."

Just then, a nurse entered.

"I'm sorry to interrupt but you have a couple of visitors here to see you."

"Visitors?" asked Olivia.

Two handsome middle-aged people poked their heads in, pushing aside the privacy curtain. The woman had a trio of mylar balloons in her grip. The man bore flowers.

"Mom. Dad," smiled Olivia.

Digger got up and backed away.

"Hello, baby," said her mother, swooping in for a hug. "We came straight from the airport." The mother was stylish, well put-together. The apple didn't fall far from the tree in that regard. The father neared the bed but remained upright. He handed Olivia the bouquet of flowers.

"Hey there, shrimp. How you holdin' up?"

"I'm good, Pop. Real good. Digger's taking good care of me."

Olivia's father turned to face Digger and offered his hand. "Russell. Glad to meet you."

"Everybody calls me Digger," he said with a firm handshake.

"Digger? Where's Clifford?""We broke up, Mom."

"Oh. He was handsome."

The visit was brief but remarkably relaxed. Olivia's folks invited Digger and her to dinner.

"Once you're done playin' hookey!" Dad joked.

Chapter 66- Meet Misty!

When Digger brought Olivia home, she was strong enough to walk on her own, but still needed plenty of rest, per doctor's orders.

Misty, Olivia's best friend, greeted Digger at Olivia's front door. Misty had the loose posture of a rag doll with small cherubic lips to match. She acted much younger than did Olivia, despite Digger's being told that they were exactly the same age.

Olivia lay upon the living room sofa and Misty sat on the edge. Digger stood guard.

"You should be in bed," Digger softly suggested.

"I don't wanna go to bed."

"I'm gonna take good care o' you, 'Livia. Digger and I." Misty turned her attention to Digger.

"Digger, you're a Gemini. Olivia, you're a Cancer. I should do your chart."

"Digger, how can you afford to take off all this time from work?" asked Misty. "No. Really."

"I taught art to some really rich kids when I was in Spain and saved up most all of the money."

"Come on. For real?"She widened her eyes. "Oh, my god. That's probably the most Gemini thing I've ever heard."

"Olivia? Are you hungry?" asked Digger

"I actually am."

"How about some chicken soup?"

"From a can? Blecch. There's a deli, not two blocks from here. They have chicken soup."

"I'm on the case." Digger kissed Olivia on the forehead. "Need anything else? Misty, I'm picking up a pastrami for myself. Anything for you?"

"A reuben and a root beer! Uh, please."

With that and a nice to meet you, Digger left the apartment.

With Digger gone, the two girls were free to dish.

*

When Digger returned, Olivia was asleep, still on the couch. Misty was watching Jerry Springer on mute.

He quietly unpacked the box of deli treats onto the dining room table. Misty got up and assisted him.

"That was sweet of you to go get soup."

"Don't be silly. Anybody would have," said Digger matter-of-factly.

"Not that Clifford."

"Oh, him."

Misty looked at Olivia as she slumbered. "Poor thing. She's been through a lot. First, the thing with Clifford running off with her money, and now the sepsis thing."

"Wait a minute," said Digger, suddenly enraged, "What do you mean, running off with her money?"

Chapter 67 - I Know That Guy

Olivia wore one of Digger's collared shirts as she finished her Sunday breakfast, seated at the table in Digger's kitchenette. Sunlight through the window made the whole room a lemony yellow. Looking about 90% back to normal, she lazily flipped through the pages of the LA Weekly.

"The Weekly says there's an auction at Sotheby's Los Angeles. Let's go!"

"You gonna buy some 'spensive art?" Digger asked in a jokey voice. "Gonna hobnob wit' da well t'do?"

"Come on. It'll be an adventure. I'll buy you lunch. Let's see how the better half lives." She rose from her seat and nuzzled Digger. "Puh-lease."

"Free lunch? I'm in."

Digger went to his closet to choose something to wear. Hmmm. What to wear at an art auction… He flipped through some of the fine clothing he had acquired in Spain.

Digger suppressed a chuckle when he saw the suit he'd had tailor-made three years ago for the Chicago art forgery swindle. Feeling cheeky, he yanked the suit off the closet bar. *Why not?*

*

Digger and Olivia signed into the large register before moving on to find seats. The auction house's main room was not as big as Digger had imagined. The walls were completely covered in heavy drapes. Blockish security guards manned each door and sensitive station. The jewelry that hung from the necks and dangled off the wrists of these people was obscene. There was old money, new money. Forget the art. A stick-up man could find himself retiring after fleecing this crowd.

Digger gasped. Melman was there.

Not only was Melman there. Clive was there, Chicago Clive, the one from the con job.

*

"What is it, Clive?" asked Melman, looking around to see if any of his rich acquaintances were noticing him. They were standing in the back of the auction room, near the sign-in books.

"This whole scene. There's something about it. Gives me an itch," complained Clive.

"Oh, come now. There is no need to feel intimidated."

Clive had just gotten back from wrapping up some messy loose ends in Nevada for Robert Werner Sr., his boss, and now he was here to scope things out, should Mr. Werner wish to liquidate some or all of his son Bobby's art "collection." Maybe he could even make some useful connections.

What made things sticky was that Bobby was always sloppy, buying things that might have been stolen or fakes. Both Werner Sr. and Clive hated it when Clive was being used as his errand boy.

"No," Clive said, as clearly irritated with Melman as he had been in Chicago three years ago. "It's not that. It's reminding me of something. I just can't put my finger on it."

Clive saw a sharp young couple taking a pair of aisle seats. Something about them jogged his memory and reminded him of that Matisse business a few years back, when he and Melman met some sketchy characters to buy many undiscovered Matisse drawings.

He finally thought to himself, *What's it to me? No skin off my nose. Even if it were the actual guy, what would I care?* But, it wouldn't leave his mind.

The young man turned his full back to Clive and, just then, something clicked.

"You! Wait!" Clive yelled across the crowd.

The young man grabbed his female companion's hand. They ducked into the crowd and toward the exits.

"I know that guy," Clive muttered to himself.

Clive chased the couple unsuccessfully through the crowd. They simply vanished.

Clive stood there for a moment while security spoke into their walkie-talkies.

He then ran to the back tables and snapped photos of the open sign-in book with a Minox B spy camera before he was chased out by security for causing a ruckus and breaking the "no photography" rule.

Chapter 68 - Meet the Parents

Of course, they drove together. Olivia wanted Digger to drive her car. He guessed that her Mercedes fit the restaurant's dress code better than his Cabriolet might.

"It's your car. Why don't you drive?"

"Because, I am a lady and I wish to be waited on," purred Olivia.

"Right away, Ma'am."

Digger pulled up to the parking valet and got out of the car while it was still running. He skipped over to the passenger side and opened the door for Olivia.

"You nervous?" Digger asked.

"Yes, actually."

Digger offered his elbow and she took it. They entered the restaurant looking fabulous. Olivia's hair was up and she wore a gown. Digger wore Armani.

The trim host said, "Ah, this way, please," and led them across a large dining room where Russell and Trudy, Olivia's parents, were waving them over.

They joined her folks at their table with an exchange of greetings, hugs and handshakes.

The sommelier approached them to take their drink order.

The elders ordered a bottle of wine for the table.

"You drink wine, don't you, Digger?" asked Trudy.

"On occasion," Digger smiled.

"Wine? I'm having scotch," said Russell. "What'll you be having?"

Digger figured that although he was driving tonight, they would probably be at dinner for at least a couple of hours.

"White Russian," Digger answered. This answer seemed to please both Olivia and her father.

Diplomacy, that's the name of the game, Digger coached himself.

"So, Digger, where'd you graduate from?"

Digger felt his spine tighten.

"I studied some at Design Center and just got back from teaching drawing and painting in Spain," offered Digger. "That, some college, as well as some private study."

"Spain, eh? That sounds wonderful," said Trudy, as if he had said, "I made the casserole myself!"

"So you didn't graduate," concluded Russell.

"He's a teacher and a skilled professional, Dad."

"I never said that he wasn't."

The waiter came and took their orders, clockwise around the table, Trudy, Russell, Olivia then Digger.

"You ordered the chicken with cream sauce and asparagus," commented Russell. "Good choice!"

Digger had no idea what to make of the dad. He felt like a hockey goalie, trying to be ready for anything that came his way,

"Honey, why didn't you call us?" Trudy turned to Digger. "It was Misty who let us know that Olivia was sick."

Olivia pretended not to hear this. She just sipped her wine.

"How's work, Dad?" she asked.

"Oh, you know, honey. Time marches on."

"Daddy here works for the Treasury Dept. They're working to get access to information about the offshore accounts of US citizens."

"Tell me more," said Digger, leaning in.

"You can't tell me that you're actually interested in this stuff," said Russell, signalling for the waiter to bring him another scotch.

"Fascinated, actually."

Digger listened intently as Russell rhapsodized about the Department's pursuance of legislation that would allow it and the IRS full knowledge about monies held in Swiss Bank accounts, those based in the Canary Islands or wherever American taxpayers are stashing their cash.

"Russell is a pit bull." Trudy said this with pride and a chuckle. "That's what they call him at work, The Pit Bull."

"Right now, people are stashing millions of US dollars that we can't monitor," he continued. "Money that's been laundered or otherwise just untaxed."

"Sounds frustrating," said Digger.

"You bet it's frustrating. But, we'll get there. Oh, yes we will. We'll get there." Russell sounded just a touch rounded at the edges by scotch.

"You take care of our baby girl, Digger," said Trudy.

"Or, she'll whup your ass," said Russell.

The evening went on, with stories of Olivia losing a tooth, crashing her first bicycle, taking dance lessons and riding horses over one summer.

Digger deftly avoided details about his own family.

At the dinner's conclusion, Digger asked if they should all walk out to the parking valets together. Trudy told the two of them to go on along, that she and her husband were going to sit for a few more moments. They all stood for good night embraces and slaps on the shoulder.

On his and Olivia's way out, Digger overheard Trudy ask Russell what he thought of him.

"I don't know. He seems harmless."

Chapter 69 - It's Him

Clive was in his basement back home, developing the pictures from his spy camera. Once the prints were dry, he laid them out on the table, near his bottle of beer. He ran his finger down the lists of signatures, some legible, some not. He read many of the legible ones aloud.

"Margaret Hathaway, Richard Hathaway, James... something."

Clive squinted and stopped when he read what looked like "Digger."

"Digger? Damn hippies."

Clive took a swig of his beer and then muttered "Time to hit the hay."

He carried his beer back up the basement stairs and turned the light out.

Once in his bedroom, Clive stripped to his boxers and climbed into bed. He closed his eyes and did a breathing exercise to help him fall asleep.

Hours later, he tossed and turned until, Bam! It hit him and his eyes flew open.

"Chicago."

*

Three days later, Clive climbed the stairs to the Getty. He went out to a courtyard where people were eating sandwiches from the concession stand. Clive stood for a moment until a couple of guys waved at him. They all sat down at a picnic table.

"You can pick 'em up anytime at my place," said the one wearing a sun visor and shades. The other one was on the chubby side and sported a beard.

"So," Clive began, hot with anticipation, "Are they authentic Matisses?"

"We can't say for certain that they are genuine, but we ourselves can say that they definitely could be."

"Could be?" asked an exasperated Clive.

The bearded one took over. "The materials were pretty old, consistent with Matisse's time period. Besides, these particular drawings had already been authenticated."

"Authenticated?" Clive braced himself for what was coming next.

They had called Melman.

Melman had been there when they, he and Clive, picked up the drawings in that sketchy hotel room scene. They had gone to procure them for that rich pain-in-the-ass Bobby and Melman had insisted upon two for himself.

Of course Melman said that they were legit! He owned two! Melman needed for them to be legit! He couldn't bear the thought of owning a fake so he gave his seal of approval without knowing anything for certain.

In the art world, if Melman said that a soup can was a Warhol, that soup can was a Warhol. His word was the only stamp those drawings needed.

The whole thing was bonkers.

It was time for the two guys to return to their day gig, restoring damaged master paintings for the Getty Museum.

Okay. So they were genuine Matisses. Clive still couldn't shake this feeling that he had been played.

Chapter 70 - Flickering

The small living room in Olivia's one-bedroom apartment flickered with dancing candlelight. Shadows shimmied on the walls and candlewax dribbled in salacious envy.

Olivia had made them a roast chicken dinner and now the stereo played Linda Ronstadt and Nelson Riddle's *For Sentimental Reasons*.

The poster Digger had stolen for *Cinema Paradiso* was taped up on her wall.

She and Digger swayed, holding each other close, cheek to cheek.

"Mmmmm..." said Olivia. "I could stay like this forever."

"Somebody has a birthday in a couple of days," Digger sing-songed. "Now, what to give the girl who has everything."

"You already gave me the troll doll, Digger," she joked. "I think you've done quite enough.

Digger raised his left arm and she passed under it, then they clung to each other like a blooming rose that has changed its mind.

"Everything, including an asshole boss ex-boyfriend." Digger paused. "You know, I could kill him for you," Digger offered. "It could be a birthday present."

Olivia chuckled. Then her face dropped its soft expression."You would. You would do that for me, wouldn't you?" asked Olivia.

There was always something about Digger, so sweet, so sensitive, yet so… so, *everything*. So smart, so sad, so capable of anything. He lacked the limitations of most men.

Digger just stared at Olivia. She returned her cheek to his.

"No, Digger. Let's leave him alone. He doesn't deserve that."

"Oh, but he does."

"Okay, maybe he does. I just don't want the man I love to do it."

"He's mean and rude. He lies and cheats those who trust in him. And, he hurts you."

"I need to leave Hawkins and Marsh."

"You need to leave Clifford, *really* leave him."

"You are so very right."

With that, they moved their mouths close to one another's.

Olivia nibbled on Digger's lower lip until he took her into a long, warm kiss.

Her eyes fluttered and her toes curled.

Digger slid his hand up her back and cradled the back of her head. He nibbled along her jawline and kissed her neck.

Olivia's head went back and then side to side.

She lifted her head and took to nibbling Digger's ear.

"I want you," Olivia said, not whispering.

They slowly swayed their way to the bedroom and he sat on the edge of her bed.

Olivia and Digger undressed each other.

*

After some tender and playful, aggressive and rough lovemaking, each left the bed, one at a time, to wash up. Olivia had gone first. Digger thought about what she had told him.

Clifford was rough, but selfish, as a lover. Things with Digger were very different. With Digger, they were two equal forces, each clawing their way through their passions. She felt *with him.* She trusted him, not to refrain from hurting her, but with her true nature. She wanted to be trusted with his.

With their heads back on the pillows, they chatted in smooth, low voices.

"Mmmm. You smell good, Digger. You always smell good."

Digger lay on his back, kissing Olivia's hand with his eyes closed. Olivia lay close by his side, staring at her hand.

"You are so gentle. You really love women."

"Most women."

"Your mother must have really loved you."

Digger did not respond.

"Tell me about your mother, Digger."

"I'd rather not."

"Oh?"

Digger realized that this wasn't something that was just going to go away. He loved Olivia and didn't fancy himself a liar, so he would to have to transcend his own discomfort and spill the beans.

"My mother taught me how to read when I was two."

"Two? Wow."

"She also gave me my first broken nose when I was about ten. When my father left us, I started getting all of his emotional mail. I became a lightning rod for all of my mother's anger and hatred."

"You became her surrogate spouse," observed Olivia.

"Exactly."

"But you don't seem to hate women."

"I think I was lucky in that the abusive stuff really didn't start happening until after my 'formative years.' I used to worship her. She was everything to me."

"So what's with all the Dark Digger stuff? The violent fantasies, the obsessions."

"I can't really explain it and I've given up trying. This is what I am and it is positively exhausting trying to jam my square peg into the round hole."

"You think it's from all of the abuse?" Olivia sounded like she was working out a math problem.

"No. Not really. My mother said that I've always been… Well, I used to shred her nipples when she breastfed me."

"Yikes. That explains a lot."

"I have these harsh appetites and severe reactions to situations. I want to say *inappropriate* appetites, but nature put 'em there, so how can they be so inappropriate? My relationship with women is… complex."

"Come on, Digger. Tell me."

"On the one hand, I seem to operate pretty honorably. I mean, I try to be polite, act out of integrity, but I see certain women and I want to hurt them. I see certain men and I want to hurt *them*, but it's different."

"With the women, is it sexual?"

"Yes."

Olivia took a deep breath. "Keep going."

"I don't know how much more to say. I could talk forever and probably wind up just repeating myself."

Olivia folded her arms, then snuggled closer to Digger. She stopped at kissing him.

"You know, Digger, since I was a little girl, I thought, Oh, no. I'm gonna get caught," Olivia began. "It doesn't matter that I really hadn't done anything yet. I just had my thoughts, my roaming, rambling thoughts that went far and wide."

Digger listened intently, this time with his eyes open.

"A couple of times, my mother caught me sticking things inside of myself—crayons, dolls—and just lost it. I mean, lost it. She beat me like a tambourine."

Digger nodded along, but did not interrupt.

"Whenever I would hear that something was poisonous, I wrote it down, thinking that someday, I was going to poison my mother. One day, she found this list, this list of poisons. Oh boy. She didn't hit me but she did put me into therapy. The therapist told her everything that happened in the sessions. That aspect alone really messed me up."

"Ever thought of poisoning Clifford?"

"I love you, Digger."

Chapter 71 - The Aston Briggs AIDS Foundation

Digger was wrapping up a job for another Hawkins and Marsh team when Clifford cornered him in the conference room. He spoke as though he didn't want anybody else to hear.

"Hey champ. How would you like to help out the Aston Briggs AIDS Foundation? You know, Aston Briggs, the famous tennis-playing piano smasher? We need you, man."

Clifford was clearly trying to seduce Digger by dangling the celebrity's name, but Digger was not starstruck.

"What do you mean, Clifford?" Digger was terse, clipped. "Sponsor you in some marathon?"

"Marathon? Me? No, no. I want to ask you to storyboard a TV spot for the foundation. I'll be directing it. There's no budget, so I can't pay you, but it's a good cause and can lead to other things."

"Like more non-paying gigs?"

"Come on, Digger. Don't you care about AIDS? I'll call you tonight and walk you through it."

Digger wanted to tell him to fuck off, but his switch only had two settings—not confrontive enough or too confrontive and he wasn't ready to burn this bridge quite yet. And, to tell the truth, he found Clifford to be intimidating.

*

That night, true to his word, Clifford called. Digger had been hoping he'd just sort of flake out. Clifford sent the scripts over to Digger's place by messenger.

Digger spent the whole weekend drawing three different spots for the foundation.

The main spot was a WWII-style victory parade, depicting the end of AIDS. The frames were elaborate with lots of detail: thousands of people cheering on the streets of New York with a blizzard of ticker tape swirling above their heads. Digger re-created the famous photo of the sailor kissing the girl, from memory. There were people holding signs with pictures of loved ones. People hoisting children into the air. Digger was meticulous in his construction of these scenes.

When he was finished, he went to the Kinko's down the block to shoot copies that he could marker. He thought sepia tones would really bring it home, so he stopped at the art supply store on his way back to his bungalow apartment.

Digger didn't linger. He made a straight shot right for the marker section. He grabbed a handful of sepia-toned markers then headed for the cashier.

"Excuse me? Laurie's not working today?"

"Laurie moved out of state. Something about a scary boyfriend."

Chapter 72 - In the Back, Then In the Front

When Digger was done with the boards, he called Clifford and left a message on his machine.

Clifford called back right away. Digger told him he could come pick 'em up anytime. Clifford asked if Digger could bring them by his place.

Digger'd had enough.

"You want 'em, come git 'em. You don't want to come, send a messenger."

"No, Digger. There is no budget for a messenger. Remember, every dollar we spend is a dollar that we take from AIDS treatment and research."

Digger drove them over, swearing all the way.

*

Just about a week later, Digger was in the Hawkins and Marsh breakroom availing himself of some of their bounty of snacks, when Tony the PA entered, wearing mirrored ski shades.

"What's up, Digger?"

"Looking for the trail mix, Tony."

"Above the fridge. Hey, I saw the boards for the AIDS spot. They were sweet. Yours?"

"Yessir. Guilty as charged."

"Yeah, I didn't really want to work the weekend, but I needed the dough."

"The dough? But this was a charity gig."

"Not for me, it wasn't. Clifford just wanted it for his reel. The foundation didn't even want the thing. The spots came out so bad that nobody wants it on their reel."

"Reel?" Digger asked, out of disbelief, not unfamiliarity with the word.

"You know, a compilation of clips used to show off your best work. It's like a portfolio."

"Right. Right."

Digger left Hawkins and Marsh and bucked rush hour traffic all the way home. He hit the bed the moment he entered the door to his place. Try as he might, he would not fall asleep, until he did.

Digger had a message from Clifford on his machine when he got up. *Just my luck.*

He dialed Clifford's number.

"So, did you call to offer me some more jobs where everybody but me gets paid?" asked Digger, *clearly* pissed.

"Oh, you found out about that. Well, if it makes any difference, I didn't get paid either. In fact, I lost money."

"Look, Clifford. I'm off the clock."

"Digger. This gig comes from Hawkins and Marsh. Their money. Straight time-and-a-half."

"It's not the money, Clifford. It's the fucking disrespect. It's the ugliness. It was vile. It was rude."

"This is business, Digger. We're behind the eight-ball. Do you want to help us out or not?"

Us. He meant Olivia.She'd been back to work for nearly a week. If Digger dropped the ball, Olivia would suffer.

"Give me an hour."

*

Clifford lived in these exclusive condos near the Farmers Market on Fairfax. Digger had to park quite a distance away and hike to Clifford's place, hauling his work kits.

Digger had money, yet was feeling like a slave again, a slave to his unspoken commitments.

He took the elevator up. Clifford greeted him at his door.

Digger began to set up shop on Clifford's coffee table.

"You realize, Clifford—"

"Yeah, yeah. You're billing me at time-and-a-half. I know."

"No. I was going to say that you don't seem to have a Xerox machine here."

"What about the fax machine?"

"Sorry. No dice."

Clifford tried to stretch out a kink in his neck.

As Digger laid out his pads of tracing paper, an image was visible through the top sheets.

"Whatcha got here, Dig boy?"

It was a caricature, a caricature of Clifford. The likeness was unmistakable. It had his crowbar jaw, his chin dimple and his camel's eyelashes. Spot on. Most caricatures were unflattering, but this one was downright vicious. Digger only caricatured people he didn't like.

"Hey! That's me!" Clifford tore the drawing from the pad and admired it. "I'm keeping this one. Would you sign it for me?"

Digger was livid. He hated Clifford. Clifford was a monster and had betrayed Olivia and stolen her savings.

Oblivious, Clifford continued, paying Digger little mind. He poured himself a fresh drink.

"Things are not going well for me at the agency, Dig. My job is on the line. This presentation has to be a slam dunk, a home run."

Clifford paced the floor as he dictated his ideas to Digger. His concepts were always so unnecessarily mean-spirited.

"Where's the script?" Digger asked.

"What script? We don't need no script. I'm the goddamn script. Got me?"

"Roger Wilco." Digger smacked his lips. "I'm thirsty. Got anything to drink?"

"I got pop, bottled water, Perrier, juice. Help yourself."

Digger excused himself and went to the kitchen.

When Digger was in there, he moved the block of knives on the counter to a different position, near the counter's edge.

"Why Digger? Why do you keep working for us? The director is an asshole. I'm an asshole. Why do you do it?"

"Stockholm Syndrome?"

"No, man. I'm serious!"

"Because no one will work with you assholes anymore. That leaves Olivia high and dry. That's why."

"You and Olivia. Quite the item." Clifford took another swig.

"Keep your friends close," quoted Digger.

"And your enemies closer!" finished Clifford, laughing. "Godfather, right?"

"Yeah. Olivia. She's pretty great," mused Digger.

"You ain't foolin', Dig."

"That's Digger."

"What?"

"That's Digger. Not *Dig*."

"Digger. Right. As I was sayin' she's the best." Clifford hoisted his empty glass into the air as if to toast Olivia's legend.

"You know, Cliffy. It must really, really suck to lose a woman like her."

"Don't call me that."

"Call you what?"

"Cliffy. Cliffy or Cliff or whatever. It's Clifford."

"Kinda sucks when people disrespect you, eh, Cliffy, old boy?"

Clifford grabbed Digger's shirt by the shoulder.

"Listen, you little shit. I *told* you—"

"Hands off, Cliffy Boy."

"You little worm. I'll kill you."

"Will you, now?"

Clifford pulled Digger to his feet by his shirt.

Digger gave him a hard shove. He angled his body into position facing away from the kitchen.

Clifford shoved Digger back, sending him sprawling toward it.

"You know, she hardly talks about you at all," taunted Digger.

Grunting, Clifford lunged at Digger, about to grab his collarbones like handlebars.

Digger grabbed the largest kitchen knife from the block on the countertop and kneed him in the groin.

"Clifford. I *really* don't like you."

As Clifford fell forward with all his weight, Digger plunged the knife into Clifford's chest. He heard a soft crunch as he twisted the knife upward into Clifford's heart. Clifford heaved and flailed. Digger held onto the knife like the horn on

292

a bronco saddle, following him closely, their bodies pressed together like a panini. His weight caused the knife to scramble Clifford's heart until his movements slowed and he eventually fell to the floor.

He withdrew the knife and watched Clifford bleed out.

Digger waited for his breath to return to close to normal before dialing 911 from Clifford's phone.

"9-1-1. What is your emergency?"

"I've just been assaulted by my boss. I think I killed him."

Chapter 73 - Tell Me Everything

The security camera recorded from the top corner of the interrogation room.

The grainy footage showed a young man in his early twenties, sitting in a metal police chair next to a table, all at a diagonal angle.

The young man sat with his hands on his knees. Every so often, he would twist his head to look about the room.

Two policemen entered the room wearing shoulder holsters. One remained standing. The other half sat on the table, cornering the seated man.

"Let's go over this again," said the policeman, leaning on the table.

"Clifford asked me to come to his house to work. He became irritated over the course of the job and drank. He drank more and more. He blew up and assaulted me. I defended myself. The guy's twice my size."

"Whoa, whoa. One step at a time," said the seated cop.

"You both started out seated, right?" asked the standing policeman.

"That's right."

"Now, we're gonna go through this slowly," said the leaning policeman. And they did, again and again. They tried to break Digger, to find any crack in his story, but their efforts had the opposite effect. The longer they went on, the more Digger perfected his answers to the point that he could recite his summaries verbatim without the slightest effort. His alibi seemed to be a selective version of the very truth.

The fact that Clifford "lost" Olivia to Digger was of particular interest to them.

*

Hours later, Digger and Olivia trotted slowly down the steps of the police station.

"So, what do we do now?" asked Digger.

"Well," Olivia was clearly shaken up. Regardless of the circumstances, her current lover had just taken the life of her ex-lover and boss. "It looks as though I have a decision to make."

Digger maintained silence.

"It wasn't self-defense, was it, Digger?"

"No."

Olivia stopped at the bottom of the stairs.

"Did you go over there to kill him?"

"No."

Olivia stared off into the sudden gust of wind, nodding.

"Okay, Digger. Tell me. Tell me everything."

And he did. On their walk, Digger told Olivia of his bloodlust ideation and how it wasn't a compulsion.

"It was a deliberate act," he whispered.

"So, it wasn't a 'crime of passion'?"

"Couldn't a deliberate act also be a crime of passion? What was a painting? A political novel? Some acts borne of passion can take years of patience to commit." Digger's eyes darted around. "I'm not any sort of vigilante. I merely play favorites. I like you. I don't like you. Their 'deserving it' is merely a personal preference."

"But, Digger, I have to ask. Who are you to play god?" She seemed to only half-believe the sentiment.

"Who is playing god? I could be killed at any moment, by anyone."

"Do you seek out people to kill?"

"No. Not yet anyway. I just took an opportunity that presented itself. I know that I've been lucky and I know that can't last."

"How can you live in the world if everybody who gets under your skin, or your zipper, is a target?"

A public transit bus whooshed by, momentarily drowning out their conversation.

"I am not above nor below any act," Digger continued, "I merely, once again, have my preferences. My mind goes everywhere and I'm no longer try to stop it."

Olivia let out a big breath.

"I'm gonna need some time, Digger."

Digger nodded.

Chapter 74 - In the Clear

It took some time and a couple of more sessions with the detectives, but Digger had eventually been cleared of all charges based on self-defense. However, his phone wasn't ringing anymore. No one seemed to be in the market for Digger's boards.

According to Meg, whom he phoned, things were slow all over town. Digger never thought he needed the work before, but right now he really needed something to occupy these long and torturous hours that led to maddening nights.

He checked his machine again. Olivia hadn't called.

He walked out of his bungalow and headed down Washington Pl. toward the ocean. After a few miles, he hit Venice Beach and merged with the foot traffic on the boardwalk.

A guy was selling little turtles, the size of a quarter, that came with terrariums—red-eared sliders. There were jugglers and breakdancers, girls giving henna tattoos and a bearded guy in a turban, zipping around on rollerblades while shredding on an electric guitar. He had a small amplifier clipped to his belt.

It was 98% tourists. Digger could breathe now. He wasn't home alone, nor was he saddled with the emotional chores that came with familiar company.

Reggae music played out of speakers belonging to a man selling cassette tapes out of the back of a pick-up truck, some of them bootlegs.

Digger couldn't use Olivia. He just couldn't.

Digger tossed small cash into an open guitar case in exchange for a mid-song nod of thanks. Just then, Digger saw the crowd dissipate and clear in one area. A show was about to begin.

According to the spray-painted sign, it was "The Prime Minister of Limbo." Digger stood there in front, his face unaffected by the scene around him.

This Prime Minister of Limbo sure knew how to work a crowd. He had music playing on his boom box while he barked, yelling descriptions of feats to come from his limbo bar, propped up behind him.

He had the restraint of an old-time strip tease artist, toying with the audience, passing a literal hat and building anticipation.

Ultimately, it was showtime! And the Prime Minister did not disappoint. He crawled underneath the bar with his chest up, each time surfacing to a wave of applause. He did this many times, each time lowering the bar, each time egging the crowd into a silly frenzy.

He tossed broken glass to be limboed on with bare feet!

Olivia meant everything.

The finale was that he had a member from the audience light the bar on fire before he crawled under it, at its lowest point ever.

The Prime Minister did it and the crowd burst into applause. He leapt up and greeted the audience, hat in hand. Digger tossed in a fin, then walked away, disappearing into the crowd of tourists.

Chapter 75 - Clifford's Funeral

Olivia recognized the absurdity of it. She wished that Digger were here with her. That was absurd. She was mourning the death of her former boss and lover, wishing that his killer were by her side. Absurd.

She drove by herself, given that she was likely not the most welcome person to attend Clifford's funeral.

Olivia merged with the procession and followed it to the cemetery.

She parked her Mercedes and left it without locking it. She'd brought flowers.

Most of the family avoided Olivia, even though she had been warmly welcomed and well-liked by them just a few months earlier. She thought it best to remain in the back of the ceremony, lest her presence cause a scene.

But, it did cause a scene.

Clifford's mother, assisted by his sister, approached Olivia.

"You just had to come," the mother said. "Your new boyfriend killed my son and you have the *gall* to show up here. Where is he? Why isn't *he* here? Where is your murderer boyfriend?"

Olivia was tongue-tied. Something in her chest gripped her, a mixture of different categories of guilt. Most of it was that she didn't feel enough of the other kind of guilt.

"I'm so sorry, Rose."

The mother spat in Olivia's face before signalling to lead her away. The sister's face was not as angry.

Olivia left a bouquet of flowers on the casket and blew the air out of her cheeks before turning around and heading back to her car.

Chapter 76 - Returning the Matisses

Clive steered his car through the winding road that led to Bobby's house in Malibu. He could have couriered the Matisse drawings, but felt like handling this himself. Perhaps it was to give Bobby a piece of his mind.

He waved off the man servant who greeted him and popped open the trunk of the car. Clive removed the black folio of drawings from the trunk then closed it with an authoritative slam.

Clive made his way down into the bowels of the earth, descending the stairs that led to the house's underground stories.

He found Bobby sitting in one of his huge recliners across from a huge TV that played the french film *Vagabond* on mute, while Carla Bley blared on the stereo.

Bobby was swirling a screwdriver in an enormous brandy snifter, seemingly lost in thought.

"Wake up, Bobby," said Clive. "Here are your drawings."

"My Matisses!"

"Whatever. Look, Bobby. I'm through running your little errands for you. Got it?"

"You work for my family, Clive, and when one of my family needs you, you will accommodate."

"I'm telling you, off the record, that this nonsense ends now."

"What do you think my father would say to that?"

"Bobby, he'd probably slap me on the back. You know he'd never fire me."

"And I'll never stop being his son."

Clive wanted to take middle-aged Bobby over his knee and give him an open-handed "lecture."

"Will that be all?"

"You may go, Clive."

Back in his car pulling out of the driveway, Clive gripped the steering wheel like it was Bobby's neck.

Clive knew that some things were just never going to sit right with him.

Chapter 77 - Someone to Watch Over Me

Olivia put Blossom Dearie on the stereo. *Someone to Watch Over Me* spilled into the air.

She felt sick to her stomach, like she had ingested a gallon of pool cleaning chemicals.

Digger, she was sure, was the love of her life, if such a thing ever existed. But, where does one draw the line? Does love trump all or was it subject to the laws of the land? How selfish was selfish? Was Digger a monster? Surely, a monster needed love, deserved understanding. His actions should have offended her more, she thought.

Olivia could not bring herself to dress, so sweats were the dress code for the day.

She peered out the window and wished she had a pet, something to cuddle, something to soothe her. Digger's place had cats. Digger soothed her. She felt grounded when he was around. He put her at ease.

What kind of person was she to think these thoughts? This wasn't her first acquaintance with her more detached self. She experienced a whole rainbow of feelings, but seemed to be able to adjust the volume on any of them.

She knew what it was like to love Digger, or did she? Did his killing Clifford change anything? Everything? Was she merely conditioned to wring her hands over a situation like this?

Olivia changed out of her sweatsuit.

She looked in the White Pages, then got into her car.

*

The stacks and stacks and rows and rows of cages excited her at first. She was getting to pet all of the shelter cats and dogs she wanted to. This excitement quickly gave way to a heavy sadness about the possible fates of these creatures.

Olivia first went into the small, supervised "Puppy Room," where puppies roamed free to rumble and play. She was nearly toppled over with little doggies, all panting and wagging.

She lifted a beagle into the air. It licked her face. Although she appreciated the gesture, the lick was not a satisfying experience.

Next, Olivia entered the kitten area. This was kitty prison, with its walls of cages. Little Polaroid snapshots accompanied each cage, listing the name of the cat inside.

A woman with no make-up, a long straight ponytail and aviator glasses approached Olivia.

"You can remove them from the cage to hold them, pet them inside of the cage, but we ask that you not set them on the floor."

"Got it," said Olivia, sliding one of the cages open. No make-up woman left to take care of something, leaving Olivia alone with the cats. Some of them mewed, pawing between the wire bars of their confines. Some cowered into corners.

Olivia made kissy sounds, but many were just too afraid to come near.

She lifted a graphite grey young cat out of a cage and its body drooped toward the floor like a towel. She held her in her arms. The inscription beneath her Polaroid image read, "Isadora."

305

Isadora purred more and more loudly as Olivia scratched her behind the ears and under the chin. No make-up returned.

"Oh man, she just loves you," the woman said.

"What kind of a cat is she?" Olivia asked.

"Russian Blue. You've *got* to take her now. Russian Blues only bond with one person. Look at you two."

Isadora butted her head underneath Olivia's chin and pushed it all around.

The shelter provided Olivia with a used pet carrier that had been donated by a patron, a litter box and litter, and some food to get her started.

On the drive home, Olivia kept her right hand in the carrier, steering with her left.

Who was she kidding? She knew who she was and, perhaps more importantly, who she wanted to be.

*

Early that night, Digger lay on his bed, fully clothed. His phone rang and he bolted right up. Whoever it was, it was good news. Anything to break the silence of the night.

"Uh, hello?"

"It's me," Olivia said. "I have some things to tell you."

"Okay," said Digger, steeling himself. "Fire away."

"No. I want to see your face."

Digger suggested dinner, but Olivia said no.

"I'll come over," said Digger.

"See you here, then."

Digger hung up then took a hurried three-minute shower. On the phone, Olivia's voice sounded impossible to interpret. Was this good news or bad news? Was this the kiss hello or the kiss goodbye? Aloha meant both. Digger's anxiety was red-lining. He was coming out of his skin.

He left his apartment and climbed into his car. His stomach was in knots as he started it up.

When he got to Olivia's place, the door was ajar. He entered.

She was sitting on the sofa, wearing a pair of college sweats. She had a cat in her lap.

"Wow. I guess things *have* changed," Digger half-joked.

"Just got her. Her name's Isadora."

The kitten stood up, arched her grey back in a stretch, then laid back down.

"Happy 26th birthday."

"Thanks. I know that you love me, Digger. I don't have to ask."

"I love you, Olivia."

She smiled politely.

"I know who and what you are. And, I also know who and what I am."

"Olivia, I will do anything, anything you ask. I ask nothing in return."

"I choose you. I'll stay with you, Digger." Olivia stroked Isadora, then looked up at Digger. "But, I can't lie for you."

"Wouldn't ask you to."

Olivia became wistful. "You should really go back to Design Center. You're just too good."

"You know, maybe you're right. I may get back to painting," Digger acquiesced.

"Be good for you. Keep that big brain out of trouble." Olivia faced Digger.

Isadora landed on the floor with a soft thud, then headed for her food.

"I'm not dumb and I'm not naïve." said Olivia. "I think I know what I'm getting myself into."

"Think so?" Digger took her by the hand. "You know, today *is* Thursday."

"Yes?"

"Would the lady like for me to take her dancing?"

About the Author

Stephen "Burpo" Debonrepos was born and raised in Southern California, where he worked as a storyboard illustrator for the Television, Motion Picture, and Advertising industries.

He is a graduate of Art Center College of Design and Mount San Antonio College.

He is the author of the graphic novel CRUSH for Aeon Press as well as the volume of self-published poetry New Old Stuff, available on Amazon.

He lives in Southern CA with his fantastic wife and their cats.

If you enjoyed this book, we would appreciate it if you could take a moment to leave a review on Amazon.

Other Books by the Author:

GIFTED

https://bit.ly/43LNlaI

NEW OLD STUFF – Poems

https://bit.ly/3K24s1n